TALES
OF
BYZANTIUM

A SELECTION OF SHORT STORIES

EILEEN STEPHENSON

For Nancy -
Enjoy !
Eileen Stephenson

Eileen Stephenson
Rockville, MD
www.eileenstephenson.com

Publisher's Note: Tales of Byzantium is a work of historical fiction. Apart from the well-known actual people, events, and locales figuring in the narrative, all names, characters, places, and incidents are a product of the author's imagination or are used fictitiously. Any resemblance to actual people, living or dead, or to businesses, companies, events, institutions, or locales is completely coincidental.

Book Layout ©2013 BookDesignTemplates.com
Cover Design: Jennifer Toney Quinlan

Tales of Byzantium / Eileen Stephenson. -- 1st ed.
ISBN- 13:978-1511741507
ISBN- 10: 1511741503

To Kenneth

This world ... ever was, and is, and shall be, ever-living Fire, in measures being kindled and in measures going out.
—Heraclitus, c. 480 B.C.

Ceremony of the Emperor

The Great Palace, Constantinople, 928

Helena sat sewing next to her sister-in-law, Sophia, in the palace's women's quarters, the gynaeceum. She stretched her legs out, feeling cramped on the short stool she was relegated to as junior empress. She stifled a bored sigh and glanced sidelong at Sophia, eyeing the elevated chair the shorter woman sat in by right as the senior empress. Sophia's plump ankles dangled just above the floor. Sophia, five months into her pregnancy, looked even more lethargic than the rest of the court ladies on that warm late summer day.

"Helena, you really shouldn't stretch your legs out so far. You'll trip someone," sniffed Sophia, stirred from her torpor at this opportunity to correct Helena. The sharp edge of the older woman's domineering voice almost scraped against Helena's skin.

Sophia's correction might have been needed if someone had been walking in front of her then, but as no one was passing at that moment, it hardly seemed necessary. Helena murmured an apology, pulled in her legs, and bent her head to her needlework. She counted it as at least the third trivial criticism that day. If it was not her legs stretched out, it was a strand of her red-blond hair coming loose or crumbs in her lap.

Sophia's pregnancy at the age of thirty-four, after only two children and many failed attempts, left her testier than usual. Worries for her daughter, wed a year earlier to the Bulgarian emperor, had not improved her disposition. Helena's father and brother, the Emperors Romanus and Christopher, were in the east trying to drive off the Persians, leaving the Augusta Sophia as the senior family member in their absence.

Both women were empresses, as both were married to emperors—Sophia to Helena's older brother, Christopher, and Helena to Emperor Constantine—but Sophia carried the title of the senior empress and augusta. Helena thought that was out of order since it was her husband, Constantine, who had inherited the throne when he was a child. Romanus Lecapenos, Helena's father and then admiral of the imperial fleet, took control of the empire from Constantine's feckless pack of regents years later. Romanus had elevated his daughter-in-law to augusta and senior empress after his wife's death six years ago.

Helena had infrequent contact with her husband. He tended to reticence in the company of his wife and her boisterous father and brothers. She had never heard him complain about his tertiary status—ranking behind Romanus and his oldest son Christopher, but ahead of Helena's two younger brothers, Stephen and Constantine. While the empire had often had more than one emperor, for one reason or another, Helena wondered if it had ever had so many as the five now clustered on its throne.

A palace eunuch entered the room, bowing repeatedly as he approached the Augusta Sophia.

"My lady, a messenger has arrived from Bulgaria with urgent news. Will you receive him?"

Sophia paled and her hand trembled at the announcement. Her daughter would have given birth in recent weeks.

"Yes, show him into my reception room. I'll receive him there," she said, a tremulous tone to her voice.

Helena rose with Sophia, offering her arm to lean on as they made their way down a corridor to hear the news. Sophia, pregnancy amplifying her already plump girth, dressed in a fine red silk dalmatica embroidered with a profusion of green leaves, and with numerous gold bracelets jangling on her arms, looked to Helena like nothing so much as a large pomegranate as she waddled down the hall.

"God willing, she and the child are well," Sophia whispered.

Helena glanced down at her worried sister-in-law, patting her arm. "I am sure they are, and no need to worry."

"Peter, Emperor of all the Bulgars, announces the birth of a son, Boris, for him and his wife, your daughter. The child was born ten days ago, and mother and son were in good health when I left," the herald announced.

The news was everything Sophia could have wished for. Sophia visibly relaxed, her face glowing at the happy tidings. She nodded to the eunuch in attendance to reward the herald generously.

Helena felt relief, too, at hearing of her niece's successful delivery. Marie was only two years younger than she was, and they had been more like sisters than aunt and niece.

Sophia, unburdened by the herald's news, walked unaided by Helena on their return to the gynaeceum.

"See, I told you there was nothing to worry about," Helena said confidently as they walked. This shared joy might be the start of a friendship between them.

"Of course, there was much to worry about. You wouldn't know; you've never had a child," came Sophia's stinging response.

Helena slowed as they reached the entrance to the gynaeceum, wondering what she had done to deserve such condescension. Only an idiot would not realize the dangers a woman faced in childbirth; she had only been trying to ease Sophia's worries. She hung back a moment, trying to regain her aplomb, and almost missed Sophia's final muttered remark.

"And if I have anything to say about it, you never will."

***

Helena lay in her bed that night, kicking herself for not seeing what had been in front of her face all along. Her father had married her to Constantine as a stepping-stone to the throne. Now that he was emperor, he must want only his sons and their children to succeed him. She and Constantine no longer mattered. In fact, if she and her husband had children, they would, by rights, come before her brothers and their children, which explained Sophia's remark. She wanted no competition for her own son, little

Michael. There could be no other reason why her father had never allowed them to consummate their marriage, though Helena was now eighteen and had been married nine years.

Helena tossed angrily in her bed. Her overbearing sister-in-law wanted nothing more than for Helena to fade into the background, childless and unimportant. Her place in the palace could only be secured if she had children. In the dark, she considered her possibilities and began to form a plan.

***

It might have been difficult to find a way to extricate herself from Sophia's company the next day since Helena was always expected to be with Sophia. But Sophia's son, five-year-old Michael, had taken ill and cried for his mother to sit beside him.

The Great Palace complex held dozens of buildings, some dating back to the days of Emperor Justinian, others of more recent vintage. In the nine years of their marriage, Helena had spent almost no time with her husband and had no certain knowledge of which building he lived in. It took her some time and judicious questioning of the various servants scurrying about its premises to finally locate the garden where her husband was ensconced.

Helena rarely encountered Constantine—just at court ceremonies and in processions to and from the Great Church of Holy Wisdom. In all the years of their marriage, they had never spent time alone together. Helena had never wanted to before, although she always expected some day they would. Constantine had been a gawky boy of fourteen when they wed, thin and pimply with shaggy black hair half covering his face. He had contrasted poorly when seen beside her robust, energetic father and her vigorous, much older brother, Christopher. Even now at twenty-three, he rarely went riding or hunting and had never used a sword, unlike the men in her family.

Helena, accompanied by her maid, stood in the shade of the peristyle surrounding the garden of the building to which Constantine was consigned. Her plan of enticing her husband into her bed seemed more daunting now, confronted with this man she barely knew, than it had in the night. She almost retreated to the gynaeceum before the memory of Sophia's callous remark returned her resolve.

She motioned to her attendant to wait on a bench along the palace wall and stepped onto the yellow brick path leading to where Constantine sat, bending over something. The soft rustle of her silk skirt caught his attention and he looked up, blinking in surprise at seeing her.

"Good day, my lord husband," Helena said as she dipped into a low curtsy.

He stumbled to his feet, putting aside the portable desk he had been using before responding, "Good day to you, Lady Helena."

They stood awkwardly, staring at each other before Helena stammered out her excuse for this first visit to her husband's environs.

"My nephew, Michael, has taken ill and desires his mother's company, so I thought I might call on you today. It has been some time since I saw you and . . ." Her voice drifted off, unsure of how to explain her sudden appearance. She had forgotten to plan exactly what excuse she would give for this intrusion.

Constantine looked at her with a puzzled expression on his face. For the first time, she really looked at this man she had been married to for half of her life. He had become an attractive, even desirable, man—a head taller than she was with a full dark beard and intelligent blue eyes. Helena could see in those eyes that he was trying to discern her purpose for being there.

Finally, he spoke and gestured to the bench where he had been sitting.

"Please, sit down. I'm just working on a drawing. Jacobus?" he called, and a eunuch with a mischievous face and ready smile appeared at his elbow.

"Here, sire." The beaming man bore a tray with a pitcher, cups, and apples.

"Could you bring—?" Constantine broke off, looking confused. "Oh, you already have something."

"Yes, sire. I saw the empress, your wife, approaching and thought you would want to share some refreshment with her." Jacobus set the tray down on a table, bowed, and slipped away.

Constantine looked after his servant with a raised eyebrow before shrugging and turning back to the wife he had been forced to wed. He sat down awkwardly at the far end of the bench from Helena.

Helena wondered what to say next. It did not seem appropriate to simply come out and say, "It's time we went to bed so I can get with child and not have to put up with Sophia so much." So much bluntness might scare this reclusive man away. Instead, she latched on to the one item he had mentioned.

"You said you were drawing. What have you been drawing? May I see it?"

He frowned slightly. "It's nothing, really. Just some pictures I will use to illustrate court ceremonies."

His words perplexed Helena. "Court ceremonies? What do you mean?"

Constantine bent over his sheets of parchment, small pots of paints, quills, and brushes, tidying the assembled implements. He was dressed in a simple but formal tunica with the imperial purple sandals on his feet. Helena's father and brothers, when not on court business, dressed in the short tunics and braccae favored by the peasants they had grown up with.

"Each court ceremony has a prescribed order. If they aren't followed properly, it can lead to confusion. I've written down descriptions of the order each should be in to eliminate that confusion." He spoke with a calm dignity that quashed any amusement Helena felt at the risible idea of writing down the order of court ceremonies, much less illustrating them.

"Hasn't anyone ever written this down before?" she asked.

"Not in centuries. Most are passed down by word of mouth. It's a problem with a change of minister or if a ceremony occurs infrequently. If performed incorrectly, it reflects badly on the empire. Also, there are certain protocols for how the rulers of other peoples are to be addressed—archon or king or emperor or emir. The Persian emir would be insulted if addressed as an archon of the Pechenegs. Wars have started with less reason," he finished drily.

Helena was intrigued by this lesson in court ceremonials. She had been empress for nine years and found the ceremonies tedious, something to be endured. Perhaps she should have paid more attention.

"I'd never thought of court ceremonies that way before," she said.

He gave a slight shrug and inclined his head to her. "You have never been taught about them. My own father, before he died, explained many of them to me."

He poured the dark wine into two exquisite rock crystal cups carved with a vine-and-leaf pattern and handed one to her. She sipped pensively and slid closer to the center of the bench where his drawings lay.

"May I see your drawings? I'd like to see how these ceremonies should look."

Constantine frowned, unused to anyone else viewing his efforts, but he picked up a sheet and handed it to her.

"This one is finished. It depicts a ceremony for a visiting ruler who is almost the equal of the Roman emperor, such as the emir of Persia."

She glanced over the parchment filled with its small painted figures.

"Is there one for a ruler equal to the Roman emperor?" she asked absentmindedly.

"Of course not." He looked startled. "We have no equal in status in the world."

Helena blushed; she should have known that. She turned her attention to the drawing. The colorful images depicted an emperor, court officials, eunuchs, and a finely dressed visiting entourage. The visitor appeared much like a Persian visitor from sev-

eral years past, one of the court officials re-
sembled the herald who announced all visitors, and a eunuch in attendance bore the
impish face of Jacobus, who had attended
them that day.

She smiled in delight at recognizing so
many of the figures, but then her gaze returned to the figure of the emperor, who
bore no resemblance to any of the five now
crowding the throne.

"I can see where you got your inspiration
for many of the people you've drawn, but
not for the emperor. Who does he resem-
ble?"

"I drew him from my memory of my father," Constantine said in a muffled voice.
He turned back to finish packing up his
tools and the drawings he had worked on,
his jaw set tight.

Helena looked up from the drawing, embarrassed she had asked. Still, there was no
way she would have known what old Emperor Leo looked like. Her husband may recall his father, but few others would around
Romanus Lecapenos.

"I think your picture is beautiful. You
have a talent for drawing; the people look

almost real, and the colors are so vibrant. Have you others I could see?"

He stood up, eyes dark, appearing ready to leave the garden.

"None I've finished yet, my lady," he said, cutting short their conversation.

Helena rose too, disappointed to see the meeting end so soon.

She reached out and laid a hand on his wrist. "Perhaps another day, then. When you've had time to finish them." Constantine would not meet her eyes.

She dipped into a curtsy and turned to leave. The maid attending her stood by the door, chatting amiably with Jacobus, but left to join her mistress. It may not have been the most propitious encounter, but they had to start somewhere.

***

That evening, Jacobus served Constantine dinner in the undistinguished palace building he lived in, a minor dwelling built by Constantine's grandfather, Emperor Basil. Emperor Romanus dwelled in the grand Boukoleon Palace while Emperor Christopher's was the older but still exquisite Daphne Palace.

"The empress, your wife, is a comely woman," said Jacobus, trying to approach the subject with tact.

"I suppose," Constantine said morosely as he forked an olive on his plate. "But she's still one of them, and I've had enough of Romanus Lecapenos and his ravenous brood. I cannot imagine why she sought me out today."

"I don't know," Jacobus said, pausing before continuing in a casual vein. "But her maid told me that the Augusta Sophia picks on Lady Helena all the time. Maybe she just wanted to get away from that."

Constantine snorted. "If that's the case, I wish she'd find someone else to pester." He scowled while contemplating his wife's visit. "I suspect Lady Helena decided to pay me a visit today for some other reason. She wants something from me, just like her family always does. There's just not much left of me to take."

Jacobus arched an eyebrow at his master's cynicism. Romanus had turned Constantine into a shadow emperor over the past nine years. Even his image on the empire's coins showed him as a beardless child rather than the grown man he was. Constantine still lived and was in good health, though, which was more than some of his predecessors in similar situations could say. Jacobus had grown fond of this solitary, bookish emperor who wielded a paintbrush and quill instead of a sword, and whose solitude cried out for a companion.

Constantine peered out of a window to his view of the blue-gray waters of the Marmara beyond the city's seawalls, eyes unfocused, drumming his fingers on the table. A rueful grin of realization spread across his face as he shook his head in seeming disbelief.

"There's one thing left they haven't taken from me. I think that's what she—or maybe her father—wants."

"What is that, sire?" Jacobus asked. He had his suspicions but kept his own counsel.

"Something I have no intention of giving her."

***

Helena's next opportunity came a few days later when Sophia took to her bed, complaining of fatigue from her pregnancy. Accompanied, as always, by an attendant, she made her way to Constantine's palace. Jacobus happened to glance out the window as she approached and escorted her up to the room where Constantine worked on his book of ceremonies. The spacious room had a row of windows overlooking the garden, next to which sat Constantine at a desk, quill in hand, parchment before him.

"Good morning, my lord husband," Helena said, as though they were accustomed to seeing each other.

"Ah, good morning, Lady Helena." Constantine's face lacked the wide-eyed surprise he had shown on her previous visit. He gave her a tight-lipped smile conveying more irritation than welcome.

"Augusta Sophia did not require my company again this morning, and I thought to visit to see if you had finished any more of your drawings."

Constantine studied his wife while considering a response. The thought flitted through his mind that Jacobus was correct—his child wife had become a comely woman. However, she was still the daughter of the man who had bullied his way onto the throne, treating his son-in-law, the rightful emperor, as some sort of a half-wit invalid.

He realized she had been looking at him for a response; perhaps she thought he was that half-wit after all.

"No, I've set the paint pots aside for a few days. I've been writing out the order of the ceremony for greeting foreign dignitaries."

"Oh, to go with your drawing," she said as she approached his desk.

"Yes, but the ceremony involves much more than just what happens in the picture. As you know, there are ceremonial robes for the emperor and court officials, the crown the emperor wears, which room to use to greet them, who attends him on the dais when the visitors are presented. It all has an order to it that preserves the empire's dignity as supreme in the world."

Helena peered over her husband's arm at the parchment on the desk, neatly inked with his words.

"If you'd like, I can read it to you," he said and began to recite the words she could have read without difficulty, a hint of sarcasm in his voice.

Helena blushed. Her educated husband was implying she could not read, as her father could not, or would not if it were not a military dispatch. Perhaps she should have been used to being treated like a feather-headed fool, the way her father and Christopher treated her. This time, though, anger burned through her at being patronized. She stepped back from the desk, eyes hardened and small chin jutting out.

Constantine looked up at her, pleased at her obvious irritation. Thinking to finish off any plans the girl had for his seduction, he condescended, "Am I reading too fast? Should I speak more slowly?"

Helena shook her head. "No, thank you. I understood it all." She made a small curtsy and strode out just as Jacobus was about to enter with refreshments.

Jacobus stood at the doorway, stunned by Helena's hasty departure. He glanced at Constantine, who stood with arms crossed over his chest, a look of harsh satisfaction on his face.

"No need for all that," he said, waving at the tray. "She's gone; maybe this time she won't be back."

"What happened?" His servant glanced disappointedly in the direction Helena had fled.

"She looked insulted when I read what I had written to her." Constantine shrugged and returned to his desk. "I don't expect she can read any better than her father does."

Jacobus listened as the footfalls of Helena's departure faded.

"She can read. I know she can. I still worked in the gynaeceum when her mother was alive. Her mother made sure the empress, your wife, could read."

Constantine peered over at his servant before turning back to his work.

"Well, perhaps I was rude to imply she could not read, but it doesn't matter. I just want her to stop bothering me."

"Sire, may I ask why? She is your wife after all."

Constantine looked at the eunuch through narrowed eyes. "Jacobus, do you know any other servant would speak to me the way you do? I'm not sure why I put up with you."

The eunuch gave a halfhearted grin. "Because you have no one else as loyal to you as

I am, that's why. So why do you want her to leave you alone?"

The emperor raised his voice in frustration. "Isn't it obvious? For one thing, her father does not want us together; if he did, she would be living with me now instead of with her brother and his wife. Any other girl her age would be living with her husband. For another, I do not want to be tricked into bed by the daughter of the man who has relegated me to the third rung on the throne—that would be mortifying. Finally, she's not interested in looking at what I've written or my drawings. She wants me for her own purposes. She probably thinks she will be in a stronger position if she has a child, and she needs me for that. And I will not be used that way."

"It sounds like you don't want a wife or children, then. You might as well walk over to the Great Church and be tonsured now," Jacobus said flippantly. "Or you could call the surgeon and have your balls cut off, like me."

Constantine snorted at the suggestion. "Of course I want a wife and children. Just not that wife and her children. My father refused to bed his first wife, the one his father chose. I will do the same."

"She looks reasonably healthy. You could be waiting a long time if you plan to wait until she dies, as he did," Jacobus said laconically. He forbore to comment on how that worked out for Constantine's father with his complicated marital adventures, sighing as he left the room. He thought it was fine for Constantine to have his drawings and writing to occupy his time, but an emperor, even third tier, needed a wife and children. Helena was not a bad sort for a Lecapena, not like the capricious and haughty Sophia. Jacobus rolled his eyes, wondering if Constantine would wake up and see Helena for the lovely young woman she was.

***

Helena stayed away from her husband for the next few days. Her cheeks burned as she recalled his reading to her—as though she was incapable of doing so herself. Did that puffed-up man think that because he had been born in the purple room, the son of Emperor Leo, and could read and write, that he was somehow better than she was? Being able to read the instructions for a stupid ceremony was not as important as being able to lead men in battle, as her father did. After all, it was her almost-illiterate father who was ruling now, not her educated husband.

That decision lasted until Sophia's endless belittling and sniping at her reached its peak when the Emperors Romanus and Christopher returned from their Persian campaigning.

"Helena, since Constantine was not out on campaign with Christopher and your father, and he won't be at the ceremony welcoming them back, I don't think you will need to be in attendance."

Helena bowed her head in submission to the augusta's instruction, seething inside at this dismissal. She was the daughter of one of the returning emperors, and the sister of the other, and had as much right to be in attendance as Sophia did. Her only chance to be free of her petty sister-in-law was to bring her own marriage to fruition, which meant enticing Constantine to her bed. If she could put up with Sophia's belittling, then she would put up with Constantine's if that was what it took to get with child.

A few well-placed coins among the servants alerted Helena to promising spots where her husband could be found during the day. One of the servants told her of his afternoon excursions in one of the gardens overlooking the Marmara.

A basket of sewing on her arm, Helena ventured into the garden when he was sure to be there and sat on a bench some distance from Constantine. Taking up her embroidering, she began to work while making sure to stretch out a long, graceful leg.

Constantine was so engrossed in his work that he did not notice her at first. Then the flash of her red dress in the corner of his eye caught his attention, and he looked up. Helena sat on a bench in the sun, her red-gold hair falling around her face as she concentrated on her stitches, a slim ankle peeking out from beneath her dress. The artist in him wondered how to describe the colors of her—hair like the blaze of sunset and skin the pale shade of whitecaps on the Marmara. He shook himself free of those images.

"Lady Helena," he said.

His wife looked up, feigning surprise. She stood and dropped into a curtsy.

"My lord husband, I did not expect to find you here," she said. "Augusta Sophia is again fatigued from her pregnancy and did not require my company. I thought to enjoy this pleasant weather."

"Ahh," he said, giving her a skeptical glance before returning to his drawing.

Helena gathered up her courage and put down her sewing. She approached her husband, peering over his arm at the drawing he worked on. This colorful depiction was of the crowning of an emperor along with the ceremonial oils anointing him and garb he must wear. Again, this drawing of the emperor was of a man resembling Constantine's father rather than of either Romanus or Christopher or himself.

"This one is better than the last," Helena exclaimed, surprised at the graceful ambo of the Great Church he had sketched, with its black marble columns supporting it.

Constantine just shrugged at her compliment.

Helena boldly moved closer and placed a hand on his arm before saying, "I admire the way you've painted your father into these illustrations."

Constantine looked down at her hand resting on his arm and carefully moved it aside so they no longer touched. He glared directly into her eyes with the tension of a coiled snake about to strike.

"Lady Helena, I realize what you are trying to do, but I will have none of it."

Helena blushed and stepped back, stuttering, "What? What am I trying to do? I don't know what you're speaking of."

She could see the anger flashing in his eyes.

"You have no interest in me. You're here for another reason—one I can guess. But I'm tired of being used—used by you and used by your father. He trampled me in his rush to the throne and treats me as less important than his hunting dogs." The words tumbled out of him, almost spitting with white heat, years of resentment igniting. "The one thing I don't have to give your family is a child of mine. You may want a child, but it won't be from me," he finished, shaking with outrage.

She stood stunned at her husband's words. They had spent so little time together over the years; she had no understanding of his feelings about her family. She had somehow imagined Constantine would be grateful to her father for taking on the responsibility of governing. Helena flushed red, swallowing hard at this uncomfortable revelation.

Finally, before fleeing this humiliating episode, she said, "I'm sorry to trouble you, then, husband." Turning to leave, she felt ashamed at his having discerned her intent and his scornful dismissal of it.

Constantine watched Helena's retreating figure before turning back to his painting. His hand shook still, and he threw down the brush in disgust. No matter how attractive the girl might be, the Lecapeni had taken enough from him. He would not give them his children.

Jacobus, for once, kept silent.

***

Helena had no difficulty avoiding her husband over the next few weeks. They saw each other for only brief periods at court ceremonies.

Romanus always said he had only taken the throne because of Constantine's youth and the ruinous incompetence of his regents. And given Constantine's childhood sickliness, it made sense to make her brother Christopher co-emperor and provide for a stable succession. All this was true.

Yet even now, with Constantine grown and healthy, Romanus conferred only with Christopher and Theophanes, his chief minister. They ignored Constantine, treating him like her two immature younger brothers despite his birthright. Helena could sympathize with how demeaning it was to wear a crown and be ignored.

Romanus was a blunt man, even brutal at times. His harsh code of honor required unquestioned obedience from his family and the empire. At the same time, he gave unquestioning obedience to the Church. He had had her youngest brother, Theophylact, castrated to ready him for the patriarch's chair, to save him from worldly temptations. No one could say he had ruled badly or spent frivolously. He used diplomacy as much as warfare to keep their borders secure. Her niece's marriage, which had brought a peaceful resolution to the empire's problems with Bulgaria, was evidence of that.

Now, though, she recalled the perfunctory prayers said on the occasion of the death of Constantine's mother several years earlier. The woman had been packed off to a monastery when Romanus had begun ruling, never to see her son again. Any other supporters or friends of Constantine had likewise disappeared into distant provinces, if not monasteries. She began to realize how alone her husband was, ignored and friendless, and how he must feel about her father.

***

Constantine, meanwhile, began to feel remorse for his angry words with Helena. He made a habit of keeping his interactions with Romanus and his brood to a minimum, but his bothersome wife had gotten his unwilling attention. Now, for the first time, at the court ceremonies they both attended, he noticed Sophia's snide insults and recalled Jacobus's remark about the older woman's treatment of Helena. He found he could empathize with his wife's predicament.

At heart a gentle soul, he rarely spoke in anger and regretted the scathing tone he had used. He may have been justified in his anger toward her family, but Helena herself had done nothing to warrant it. Well, except to try and lure him to her bed for her own purposes—that was aggravating. Even so, he felt his words to her had been harsher than imperial etiquette permitted.

***

Weeks went by, and leaves fell as autumn began. In late October, an ambassador from the Pechenegs arrived in the city to meet with the emperor on a territorial dispute. Romanus would do the negotiating, assisted by Christopher, but there would be an elaborate ceremony in the Chrysotriklinos, the golden throne room, in which all five of the co-emperors would be in attendance, as would Helena. Sophia's pregnancy was enough advanced that she was excused.

Eunuchs maintained the exquisite silk raiment the imperial family wore on these grand occasions in great cedar closets packed with fennel leaves to prevent any damage from insects and other pests, moving them into the palace when the specific garments were needed. Servants dressed each of the emperors in a long gold-banded purple tunica cinched at the waist with a gold-link belt, and a maniakis, a heavily embroidered, gem-encrusted collar stretching over the shoulders and halfway down the chest. Each of the five emperors wore a crown, Romanus's being the most impressive with enameling and cabochon rubies and amethysts encircling it.

Helena's tunica of gold-embroidered red silk with wide Dalmatian sleeves falling almost to the ground was no less impressive. At her throat, the servants placed a heavy gold-and-pearl collar before adding crescent earrings to her ears, heavy with many tiny pearls. Finally, a eunuch placed the gold crown on her head.

Trumpeters in the throne room announced the entrance of the glittering imperial family. The waiting crowd of servants, courtiers, guests, and the Pecheneg ambassador fell silent, bending their heads and falling to their knees in obeisance. Helena's two younger brothers, Stephen and Constantine, led them in, followed by Helena and her husband, and then by Romanus and Christopher, who took the two thrones centered on the dais. Helena's younger brothers took the lower thrones to their father's left, while she and Constantine sat ensconced on thrones to Christopher's right.

A herald announced each of the various officials who approached the thrones to make their requests of Romanus. A court secretary stood discreetly behind Romanus, whispering advice to him as each supplicant approached. Helena distracted herself at these tedious ceremonies with examining the dazzling mosaics circling the walls and domed ceiling depicting the city's founder, Emperor Constantine, and the law-giver, Emperor Justinian, and his empress, Theodora. Light streamed in through the high windows sheathed in the palest alabaster panes, illuminating the dust motes dancing in the air.

Helena glanced at her husband as the monotonous conversations continued and realized he was paying rapt attention. He may only have ranked in the third place among the five co-emperors, but he treated the position with respect. She glanced over at her two younger brothers, who were squirming and giggling over some crude joke, as was their way. At twelve and fourteen, they should have behaved better. The thought occurred to Helena that she had never seen her husband conduct himself indecorously at a court ceremony the way the two boys did.

The time arrived for the introduction of the Pecheneg ambassador. The crowd parted to reveal a solitary dark figure approaching the dais. Helena thought she had never seen a man as dangerous as this ambassador to the Roman emperors. He advanced to them with the menacing grace of a panther before speaking the expected phrases of homage.

The ambassador had a swarthy complexion and stood only middling tall. Black hair flowed down his back, and his pointed beard was oiled to a shine. While unarmed, as required for all in attendance with the exception of the imperial guards, he looked as though he could kill—had killed—with only his large hands. He wore a black leather knee-length robe embroidered and beaded with the pattern of a wolf, fangs bared and tongue lolling. A silver collar surrounded his throat, and wide bright silver bracelets on his arms glinted in the light. The grim set to his mouth suggested he did not smile often, and his dark eyes took in everything—her giggling brothers, the magnificent golden throne Romanus sat on, soft and beardless eunuchs, the formidable wealth displayed by the court, and scribbling secretaries. He reminded her of a ravenous animal eyeing its prey.

The ambassador knelt before her father and spoke to Romanus in Greek with a coarse foreign accent.

"Basileus, I bear greetings from the archon of my people," the ambassador began, using Romanus's formal title. He continued on in the flowery language required of those addressing the Roman emperor before eventually getting to the issue at hand—a point of disagreement with the strategos, the military governor, of the Cherson district on a piece of land both claimed.

Emperor and ambassador took the measure of each other. Romanus, every bit the soldier the ambassador was, listened to his request, and tilted his head courteously. After a brief consultation with the court secretary at his elbow, Romanus announced his decision.

"After hearing your request, I find your appeal has some merit. However, our strategos's position on this matter is also valid. To settle this dispute, if your people still want this land, they may have it on payment of a thousand gold nomisma to the strategos. Will this be acceptable?"

The ambassador bent low, murmuring his acceptance of the offer, his cold and opaque eyes reminding Helena of a lizard's.

Romanus appeared pleased. "Excellent. My secretary will compose letters to our strategos and to your king with our decision."

Helena looked at her father, confused. He had called the Pecheneg ruler a "king," but the ambassador had named him "archon." She recalled Constantine calling him an archon, too. Glancing at her husband, she saw he was flushed with irritation at this careless misnomer.

The ceremonies for the day soon concluded, and the imperial family returned to the dressing rooms, where they exchanged their expensive garments for casual attire. Helena, distracted when the heel of her shoe caught in the hem of her dress, bumped into Constantine on her way out.

"Oh, please excuse my clumsiness, my lord husband," she stammered, not meeting his eyes. She felt a flush rise on her cheeks. She was still embarrassed at their exchange weeks earlier.

"It is nothing, Lady Helena." He looked down at Helena, uncomfortably reminded of his angry treatment of her.

Impulsively, he asked, "May I speak with you a moment?"

He guided her into an empty alcove where they could be alone.

"I wanted to apologize to you for the harshness of my words the last time we spoke. It was unkind of me."

Helena stared, mouth agape. He was apologizing to her after she had spent the past few weeks feeling guilty about how he had been treated by both her and her father. She closed her mouth and cleared her throat.

"I must apologize as well. I should have realized how you felt. It can't be easy to be pushed aside as though you don't matter."

"No," he said, a rueful frown on his face. "No, it isn't."

He looked into the hall, deserted now except for Jacobus, who was trying not to be too obvious while studying this lowly emperor and his empress. Constantine turned back to Helena, stretching out an arm to her.

"May I escort you back to the gynaeceum?"

In the awkward silence that followed as they walked the brick pathways to the Daphne's gynaeceum, Helena thought to ask Constantine about the menacing ambassador of the Pechenegs.

"You thought he looked dangerous?" he said with an eyebrow arched. "Little wonder, he is a Pecheneg after all. Do you know anything of them?"

"No more than their name. My father and Christopher do not speak of state affairs with us women. Are they so terrible?"

Constantine raised an eyebrow at her ignorance. "They are far worse than the Rus or any other Turks, even though they are related to the Turks. The Rus and Turks fear the Pechenegs more than anyone else. That land your father let them have today may have been worth ten thousand nomisma or more; but it was worth it to let them have it for only a thousand. A war would cost a great deal more."

"How have you learned so much about the Pechenegs?" Helena asked. "I know almost nothing about the empire's enemies."

The side of his mouth quirked up, amused at the question.

"My father taught me when I was very young to pay attention to what happened at audiences. That's where I started learning about them."

They reached the entrance to the Daphne but lingered in conversation.

"I've made my own notes about the various peoples surrounding the empire— Turks, Pechenegs, Bulgarians, Alans, Armenians, Hungarians, Persians, and the Franks. I have several histories written by others, too." He paused, uncertain about what she might say. "If you're interested, you may visit my library and read them."

Limpid blue eyes gazed down at her, his forgiveness of her for the sins of her father washing over her. She felt as though things were starting afresh between them.

"I would like that. Sophia's time is drawing near, and she stays in her rooms much of the day. I often have hours to fill. Thank you."

Helena gave a deep curtsy, turned, and walked up the steps to the Daphne Palace, where the doorkeeper, an old eunuch named Maurice, opened its carved cedar doors for her. She glanced back to see Constantine speaking with Jacobus as they returned to their own small palace building.

***

"The Pechenegs, although a tribe of the Turks, cause the other Turks to tremble with great fear since they have been brought close to destruction by them. Likewise, the Rus fear the Pechenegs above all others since they have often raided their lands, stealing cattle, horses, and sheep, wreaking great ruin. Therefore, the Pechenegs can hold the Turks and the Rus in check when the empire gives them enough generous gifts."

Helena read Constantine's notes with fascination. The books she had available to read in the gynaeceum were limited to the Bible and other religious writings, and to the few romantic stories favored by Sophia. Constantine's library opened a door to a world she had not realized existed.

Constantine peered over the edge of his desk at his wife as she perused his writings. Seeing her excitement at learning from them pleased him more than he had expected. His eye lingered on hair the color of golden flames.

"From what you've written, it sounds as though the Pechenegs are the most vicious enemies the empire has."

He nodded. "Yes. The rest of the Turks and the Bulgarians are closer to us and bad enough, but the Pechenegs are the worst, I think. They're never reluctant to resort to the most brutal torture or killing. So I was not surprised when you said you thought their ambassador was dangerous. They all are."

Helena looked at Constantine thoughtfully. "Do you think they would attack the empire?"

Constantine put his quill down to consider his answer. "Not now. Your father, and mine before him, kept the peace with them by sending generous gifts each year—gold, silver, silks, wine. But we can never forget they are waiting only until the empire is too weak to defend itself. When that moment occurs, God help us because no one else will. They are the worst of the worst."

Jacobus entered the room then with wine and small cakes for them to share. The two ate and drank quietly as they spoke of the Roman Empire's many complicated affairs. As they finished eating, Helena rose to leave.

"I must return to the gynaeceum; Sophia will want me in attendance."

"Of course," said Constantine. He rose to escort her out, brushing crumbs from his tunic.

Constantine escorted Helena outside into the crisp fall air, where her attendant waited. In the sunlight, he noticed a few faint freckles spread across her cheeks, and he almost reached out to stroke them.

"If you would like, I have notes on the Bulgarians and the Alans and others you can read." Constantine ran a diffident hand through his dark hair, pushing back a strand that had fallen forward.

Helena beamed up at him. "I would like to," she said. "It will depend on when Sophia has no need of my company, but I should be able to return in the next day or two."

***

Over the next few weeks, Jacobus busied himself finding delicacies to serve during Helena's many visits to his emperor—late apples, small loaves of bread spread with a lemon-and-honey conserve, olives in honey vinegar, almonds toasted with cinnamon.

Constantine, a man with a hearty appetite, did not notice the change to richer fare. Helena's interest in his writings when no one else besides Jacobus had even cared what he was doing soothed his neglected soul. Her genuine admiration for his paintings and drawings eased the feeling that his existence had become meaningless.

Helena realized that no one since her mother had died years earlier had treated her as a person with intelligence, until now. Her father and Christopher loved her but never spoke to her of important matters. Constantine had opened a new world for her.

In mid-November, Helena and Constantine sat near a brazier in Constantine's study, sipping warm spiced wine Jacobus had served.

"Tomorrow is the start of Advent. There will be a ceremony at the Hagia Sophia for it," said Helena. "Do you have a description of that one yet? Now that you have me thinking about the ceremonies, I want to be sure I do it properly."

Her husband gave her a quizzical look. "After nine years, you don't recall how it is done?" he asked with a teasing tone, nudging her foot with his.

She nudged his foot back, smiling sheepishly. "I've just done what I was told to. I never thought to be attentive. I think I've been dressed in red gowns for them."

"Yes, we do wear red, all of us, as well as the priests and patriarch. We'll process from the palace to the Hagia Sophia. The most important thing to remember is the order we are in—starting with the least important to the most important."

Constantine looked down at his cup, swirling the heated wine within. "After the court officials and senators, the women enter, and as empress, you will be the last among the women since Sophia won't be there. Your father and the patriarch will be last, surrounded by priests with many candles and much incense."

She wrinkled her nose. "Why all the worry about going in a certain order? I can understand some of it, but whether one senator goes ahead of or behind another seems silly."

Constantine reached up and rubbed his forehead before leaning forward, elbows on knees, to explain.

"The empire and all its people have a certain order to it, a certain standard. If the processions are out of order, then the people witnessing it will see the disorder and think the emperor is weak, that the empire is weak. One senator placed behind a more senior one may appear to be a small thing, but those small mistakes can lead to greater ones and to the downfall of the emperor, or even the empire."

Helena gazed at his earnest face, bemused at his intensity. The air was chilly, but she felt warm in his company.

"I'd never thought of it that way before."

"I'm sure you will do well tomorrow," he said and reached a hand out to squeeze hers. His hand lingered while he looked into her eyes, giving her a cautious smile. Helena turned her hand over so their palms touched and fingers entwined, returning that affection. The thought of how well their hands fit together hung in her mind.

"Helena, in September, I know I spoke harshly to you when I thought you were . . ." He coughed to clear his throat. He looked unsure of how to approach this delicate topic.

She nodded at him, too shy now to speak of her own desire.

He leaned in closer to her, their faces less than a handsbreadth apart, speaking so only she could hear his words. "But after nine years, like a poorly managed court ceremony, I think matters are out of order between us. It is time we were bedded."

He placed a finger under her chin and leaned in to kiss her. Helena inclined her body toward his as Constantine's arm reached around her, a yearning for him welling up from deep within her. His kiss pleaded for her acceptance, and her body gave its assent.

Constantine pulled back to look at her. She wondered if her eyes had the same eager look his did; she thought they must. Helena reached up to cup his face and said, "Yes. But when?"

He smiled and kissed her again. Helena was giddy with delight at the feel of his lips on hers, still longing for them when he leaned back into his chair.

"Tomorrow night, after the Advent ceremony. Everyone will be tired from it. I have a plan. I'll come late to your room. Just be sure you're alone."

***

The next night, two hooded figures wrapped in eunuch's robes walked the paths of the palace grounds through milky moonlight. A monastery semantron sounded in the distance, marking the fourth hour since sunset. One of the two carried a pitcher of wine, spilling a spotted trail as they walked. The other held a lantern to light their way.

"I'll go first with the wine and tell the old doorkeeper Maurice I thought he'd like to share a few cups on this cold night. I'll get him into his chamber and keep his back to the door so he can't see you pass through the vestibule." Jacobus rubbed his beardless cheek and arched an eyebrow in amusement at Constantine. "The robes help in the dark, but no one seeing your beard would mistake you for one of us."

Constantine snorted.

"You remember where I told you her room is? You are fortunate she is near the top of the stairs and Sophia and Christopher at the other end of the floor."

"I remember. How long before you think I can pass?" Constantine eyed the pink granite walls and arched marble façade of the Daphne Palace, imposing in its grandeur. He thought he saw a soft light in the window Jacobus had said was Helena's.

"Not long. Maurice enjoys his wine, and he'll be happy I stopped by."

Constantine shivered in the shadow of the small Church of St. Stephen that lay in the center of the Daphne's courtyard as Jacobus knocked and was let into the building. He waited until he felt confident the two men were enjoying the wine.

He gently opened the heavy door a few inches, listening for any sign of Maurice's attention to it. Hearing only the eunuchs' raucous laughter, he opened it wider and entered. He passed by the doorkeeper's room, slipping past without the old man noticing. His soft leather shoes made little sound on the worn marble stairs.

Constantine wondered if he had lost his mind, sneaking into the Daphne that night. The palace was his anyway by birthright, Helena had been his wife for nine years— though he had never spent a single night with her, and she was the daughter of the man who had usurped his throne; none of this made any sense. Except when he thought of her soft lips, her hair the color of sunset, the way her body had felt when she leaned against him, and even more, how he had felt when she leaned against him. Then it made the most miraculous sense.

In a shadowy corridor he had not visited since childhood, he saw the door Jacobus said was hers and knocked lightly. In an instant, he entered his wife's room.

They stood close, listening for anyone who might have awakened at Constantine's entrance, but heard only the sounds of the imbibing eunuchs. A brazier in a corner radiated warmth, and a single beeswax candle lit the room. He looked down at Helena, exhilarated at his own audacity.

She appeared like an exquisite angel in a church mosaic, dressed in a linen shift with her hair falling around her shoulders. He flung off the heavy eunuch's cloak he wore and, putting his hands around her slim waist, pulled her to him. He pressed his lips to hers in a long, slow kiss that felt like he was experiencing heaven.

He finally pulled back. "I thought tonight would never come." He was not sure whether he meant he never thought he would have wanted this night with her, or if it was the anticipation over the past day that had made the time go slowly. Now, with her warm in his arms, it did not matter.

She reached up to stroke his cheek, speaking in a whisper. "I thought of you all day. I feared you would not come."

He gave her a half smile. "Did I not say I would?"

"You did. But you were not willing a few months ago; you might have changed your mind."

"Does this feel like I've changed my mind?" he said, kissing her again, hungrily. The scent of her rose perfume filled his head while his hands pressed her hips close. He could feel her body soften in his arms, and all the pent-up desire, all the yearning for a lover surged through him like a great wind howling through the streets of Byzantium.

Without thinking, he found himself struggling to take off his clothes while somehow continuing to kiss Helena. She pulled back and stopped him with a finger to his lips.

"Husband, you've explained so many imperial ceremonies to me. Is there one for when an emperor first beds his empress?"

Constantine shook his head, not in disagreement so much as to slow the drumbeat in his head. What had she said? He bent his head so their foreheads touched and his hands gripped her shoulders, trying to slow his breath.

"Ceremony. Is there a ceremony?" He tried to catch his thoughts. "I'm not sure. There hasn't been a marriage newly consummated between an emperor and his empress since my father's time. Let me think about this."

Constantine gazed into Helena's eyes as his mind raced over what such a ceremony might be like.

"Imperial ceremonies take place in a certain room and have particular people participating in them," he murmured.

"Hmm, I think we are the only two people who need to be in this one," Helena laughed, her hand on his cheek. "And I don't know where else we could go."

"And there are special robes for ceremonies." Constantine looked down at his wife's garment. "In this case, I don't think a robe is needed." His hands reached to loosen the cord around the neck of her shift. He felt her tremble as he helped pull it over her head. Breathing became difficult as he beheld her nakedness, transfixed by her soft curves and skin glowing in the candlelight.

"What of the emperor? Does he need a robe?" she asked, a quiver in her voice. She reached up to his tunic, warm hands pulling at its cords.

"No. No, he doesn't," came his hoarse answer. They fumbled with his clothes, eager to be free of them, straining to feel their bodies touching, hands stroking, lips kissing. Finally, clothes discarded, they tumbled into the bed, jolting it against the wall in their haste.

***

Downstairs in Maurice's room, he and Jacobus had been joking about "the beards"—the men who, unlike themselves, were still whole and suffering from the pangs of carnal desire.

"You would not believe how wild those young emperors are," said Maurice, speaking of Helena's younger brothers. "Can't have a servant girl anywhere near them." He yawned and rubbed his eyes, but then he grinned at Jacobus. "Any wine left?"

"I think there is," Jacobus answered, looking pleased at the request, and poured another cup for the older man. Maurice chattered on, gossiping about the concubine Emperor Romanus had recently acquired, when they heard the sound of something moving above their heads.

"What was that?" asked Maurice, regaining some of his attention.

Jacobus arched an eyebrow and turned his head as if to listen better. There was no more noise, so he simply shrugged. "Probably just cats fighting. With all the cats around here, I'm surprised we don't see more fights."

Maurice relaxed then and leaned his head against the wall behind his chair. "Probably right. Just cats. Fighting." He closed his eyes and began snoring.

***

As dawn approached, Jacobus was becoming impatient. Maurice could not sleep too much longer, and the other servants would soon be rising. He sprang to attention when he heard the soft scuff of shoes on the stairs. Looking into the hall, he saw Constantine strolling down to him.

"Well?" he asked in a whisper, though he did not need to. His emperor had never looked happier.

Constantine, beaming, clapped him on the shoulder and said in hushed tones, "Let's go, shall we."

Once outside, walking briskly back to their own palace, Constantine said, "I hope you and Maurice are good friends. I think you'll be spending more time with him."

***

Helena lingered in bed in the morning, making the excuse to Sophia of a headache, but instead reliving every blissful moment of the time she and Constantine had spent together. She could almost be grateful for Sophia's pettiness starting her on this path. Almost.

She had never imagined a man's touch could arouse her as Constantine's had, nor had she imagined how her touch could excite such passion from him. She felt intoxicated and alive as never before, satiated and hungry.

It was hunger, but not for food, that roused her from her bed at midday when she judged Sophia would be napping, and she escaped unaccompanied by an attendant to Constantine's small palace. Once inside, a heavy-eyed Jacobus greeted her with a smile before leading her to Constantine.

He sat at his desk with parchment and paint jars on it, looking out the window as she entered. He turned to see her, and she rushed into his arms.

They kissed hungrily. Then Constantine whispered in her ear, "Thank you for the most wonderful night of my life." His hands held her close, stroking the length of her body, feeling the sweet curve of breast and buttock.

Her soft lips turned up, kissed his cheek. "It was for me as well." She laughed softly, enjoying the feel of his body against hers. She pressed closer, understanding now how desire flowed between a man and a woman. "I came alone."

Constantine grinned at her. "Did you, now? I suppose that means I must be the one to guard your virtue."

"Definitely. Where would be the best place to, uh, guard my virtue, do you think?"

"I've a room down the hall I think would be perfect for that," he said with mock seriousness. "Let me show it to you." He grasped her hand as they practically ran to his bedchamber.

***

Over the next few weeks, Jacobus almost regretted the companionship his emperor had found with his empress. The nights of drinking with Maurice took their toll the next day, and Helena's occasional solitary daylight visits to her husband seemed the height of recklessness if she meant to keep her father from learning the couple were no longer chaste.

On one memorable occasion, Helena's father had crossed her path as she was leaving. Jacobus rushed to her side, pretending to be her escort, and apologized for his slowness at joining her. Romanus gave him a cursory glance before continuing on his way.

"Thank you, Jacobus," Helena said as she watched her father continue on his way to the Augustaion and the Hagia Sophia, where he would meet with the patriarch.

"Of course, my lady." He paused. "My lady, don't you think your father should know you are, uh, spending time with your husband?"

Helena gave him a sidelong look as they walked back to the Daphne Palace. "If he knew, he would try to keep us apart. I'll wait until he has no choice but to let us live together."

Feeling philosophical, Jacobus thought that would happen soon enough.

***

The feast of Christ's nativity dawned bright and crisp after a sprinkling of snow fell during the night. The imperial procession from the palace to the Great Church of Holy Wisdom, the Hagia Sophia, left not long after sunrise, with crowds along the way even at that early hour. Once in the church, the protracted service of the Divine Liturgy for the feast day and the procession back lasted until almost midday.

The silk-lined wool robes Helena wore were no match for the cold outside, but the crush of women surrounding her in the empress's gallery in the church, as well as the crowds of men below in the nave, warmed

the inside enough that she soon found herself perspiring.

Blessedly, Sophia had not joined them.
Helena wanted no scratch of irritation to
mar her enjoyment of the day. The joyful
hymns from the eunuchs' choir reflected her
own happiness. She gazed out to where
Constantine sat, enthroned between her father and brothers, and wished it was already
night. He had promised to visit her then.

The patriarch and priests, in gold robes
with mitres crowning their heads, circled the
dais with candles and smoking censers before proceeding to the altar. There, screened
behind the shimmering silver iconostasis
that rose almost to the lower edge of the
great dome, the consecration occurred.
Gold-encrusted mosaics of Mary with her
divine Son sparkled around the church, reminding all of her importance as the mother
of Jesus on this day.

Finally, the service concluded and the
procession returned to the Great Palace for
the celebration feast. Helena hosted the
highborn ladies of the court in the Daphne
Palace while her father, brothers, and husband hosted the men in the Chrysotriklinos.
The Advent fast over, the court ladies rel-

ished the feasting of that day. Helena could nibble just a few bites while thinking only of her husband.

Impatient and desperate to escape the noise and crush of so many women for Constantine's company, Helena took the opportunity to slip out after a visit to the privy. Donning a mantle, she walked the short distance to where the men dined. The fresh air invigorated her, clearing her head.

She arrived at the great hall, her breath issuing in puffs of frosty white. From a distance, she watched eunuchs and servants passing in and out of the building until she saw one she recognized and thought she could trust.

"Demetrius," she hissed at him to get his attention.

The old eunuch looked around, confused until she caught his eye.

"I need you to find my husband and tell him I must speak with him here," she said, trying not to appear too anxious. "Please don't disturb anyone else when you speak with him."

The servant disappeared into the golden throne room, and a few minutes later, Constantine emerged, wondering what she needed.

Helena pulled him around from the side of the entrance and sank into his arms, enjoying the warmth he emanated.

"I just wanted to see you," she said. "That's all. Is it so bad that a woman should want to see her husband?"

"I think you must be the boldest woman I've ever known," he said, kissing her. "Boldest, or maybe the most foolhardy. I'm not sure which it is."

"Foolhardy is what I think it is, for both of you" said a voice behind them. "Would you mind telling me what is going on here?" Emperor Romanus glared at them.

Constantine stiffened at the sound of his father-in-law's—the usurper's—voice. A protective arm around Helena, he turned defiantly to Romanus and said, "I'm kissing the wife you gave me." Helena put a cautioning hand on his arm before he could say more.

"Father, can we talk about this?" she asked.

"I think we need to," Romanus answered, scowling at his daughter. He stood before them, red-faced and angry, his fists on his hips. He jerked his head at Constantine. "You, back inside. I'll speak with you," indicating Helena, "later."

Constantine did not move; he only glared at Romanus. He was about to speak when Helena said, "Constantine and I both need to speak with you."

Romanus's face darkened at their disobedience. In the circumstances, however, with a hundred guests waiting for him, he could not force either of them to do anything without causing great embarrassment.

His eyes darted from one to the other before he growled, "I'll see you both in the Boukoleon at sunset." With a final grunt of disapproval, he spun on his heel and returned to the hall and his guests.

"I'm sorry," Helena said. "I know you have little reason to love him, but I think he will come around."

Constantine stared after his father-in-law in frustrated helplessness. Her father, a powerfully built man and the leader of great armies, intimidated and angered her husband. Looking into her husband's eyes, she realized something else.

"Constantine, just remember that no matter what my father says or does, it is what we say and do that is the future. We are married; I am his daughter. Beloved, we will be his heirs, not my brothers."

He gave her a cynical sidelong glance. "I suppose that's possible. But have you mentioned it to your brothers?"

"I don't need to. I know it."

Helena may be Romanus's daughter, but Constantine had seen his father-in-law dispose of too many of his relations and friends. He shrugged skeptically. "Maybe. I won't let him hurt you, though. I'll take the blame for this." He reached up and stroked her fair cheek. "We need to get back to our guests now. I'll see you at sunset at the Boukoleon?"

She nodded, too full of purpose to speak.

***

Helena and Constantine waited in apprehensive silence, hands clasped, for her father to appear. Helena felt as though some of Constantine's wisdom seeped into her through his touch, and some of her strength of purpose fortified him. The sound of Romanus's resolute stride echoed down the hallway to the room where they waited.

Constantine raised her hand to his lips, kissing it as though it might be for the last time.

"So, what do you have to say for yourselves?" Romanus's voice was dangerously low as he sat down opposite them.

"I am entirely to blame for what happened between your daughter and me," said Constantine.

"Husband, that is not true. Father, I approached him first. The blame is all on my part."

Romanus scowled at them both. "Helena, I expected better from you. The marriage would have been consummated when I thought you were ready. You disappoint me."

Helena tried to keep her face calm as her father spoke, but anger rose in her.

"When you thought I was ready? And when would that be? Marie, your granddaughter, who is two years younger than I am, is married just a year and already has a child. Or maybe there is another reason why you didn't want us together? So I ask again, when would we be ready?"

Romanus turned red at his daughter's challenge, the muscles in his neck bulging out. "When I decide you are ready," he bellowed. "I am your father, and I will not rush you into the marriage bed."

Helena thrust her small chin out. "Well, I decided I was ready."

Constantine interrupted, "No, I decided we were ready; it wasn't her."

Romanus's eyes narrowed, and he wagged a finger at them, "And I can decide that you aren't ready. I'll put the two of you under guard so you can't see each other."

"And I tell you we are ready. More than ready," Helena retorted.

"No, Daughter, you aren't. Don't test me on this, or you'll regret it." His hand rose to her face, a finger jabbing at her. Romanus looked ready to burst as he rose to his feet.

Helena sprang up after him. "How can you say this to me? You've always said how important marriage is, what a sacrament it is, and important to bring children into the world. The Church has blessed our union, and you are saying, no, I can't live with my husband? After you forced us to marry?" She looked her father up and down with disdain.

"For someone who professes to be of such deep faith, your actions keeping Constantine and I apart are not those of the

Church's faithful." Her father's deep religious beliefs gave her the whip hand in this argument.

"You don't understand now. You will when you have children," said Romanus, looking embarrassed at being caught by his own words. He turned as though getting ready to leave.

"Well, that will be in about eight months, so perhaps I will then. I know I would not try to keep a wedded man and wife apart, though."

Constantine, standing beside Helena and watching the father-daughter sparring with interest, snapped his head back toward his wife, wondering if he had heard her properly. He had known she could get with child at any time, but he had imagined it might happen at some vague point in the future.

Romanus put a hand to his forehead and muttered, "Oh, God. What foolishness have they gotten into?"

"Father, I'm not foolish. I want to live with my husband and sleep in his bed each night. Starting tonight and every night. What is foolish is to try and keep us apart any longer. What will you say when people see my belly growing? You've been married, and now you have another woman to warm your bed without being married. We're married, and we're going to have a baby. Why can't we live together?"

Constantine looked between these two—the man who had forced him to drink the bitter cup of humiliation and irrelevance, and that man's daughter, who admired him and was the woman he loved. As different as they were, he had the odd sense they were two sides of the same coin—humiliation and irrelevance, balanced on the obverse by love and meaning.

"Father, please understand," Helena pleaded softly. "We love each other and want only to be together, with our child." She reached up to touch his hard sailor's face, burnt by years in the sun and wind. "Please, Father, don't keep us apart."

Romanus stood teetering on the edge before relenting.

"If you're already with child, it's too late to stop it. I'd rather you had waited, but what's done is done," he said grudgingly.

Relieved at her father's reluctant acceptance, Helena embraced him. "Thank you. You won't regret it."

Romanus glanced at his son-in-law with a disparaging look. He muttered, "Probably better to have her married to you rather than to some soldier who might beat her. She's too willful to take a husband's corrections."

Constantine half smiled at that assessment while reaching for Helena's strong hand. He would never have warm feelings for his father-in-law, but he would keep the peace for her sake.

Helena stepped away from her father and into her husband's embrace. Romanus left them then, bent before the force of their desire.

"Did you come to me this afternoon to tell me of the child?" asked Constantine. He looked into her eyes, hands circling her waist.

"Yes. I'd planned to tell you tonight, but I couldn't wait till then." Helena's face radiated happiness. "We don't need to sneak around anymore, and I don't have to spend another night under the same roof as Sophia. I will spend all my nights with you."

And so she did.

Author's Note:

Constantine VII is known to history by the sobriquet "Porphyrogenitus" (born in the purple) because he was born in the purple porphyry marble room of the Great Palace. All children born to a reigning emperor were born in that room, but his father, Leo VI the Wise, had a marital history that would rival that of England's Henry VIII. Constantine was given this particular nickname to emphasize his right to the throne. Like Henry VIII, Leo died when his only son was still a child, and Constantine, a sickly boy, became a pawn between various regents for seven years before Romanus Lecapenos took control when Constantine was almost fourteen.

Romanus had reasonable expectations that one of the three sons he had named as co-emperors would succeed him. However, Christopher, the eldest and most promising, died a few years after this story. The younger two, Stephen and Constantine, were fools who did not long survive their betrayal and usurpation of their father sixteen years after the events of this story. It was the quiet survivor, Constantine Porphyrogenitus, who ruled after Romanus, with Helena sitting beside him as empress and augusta. The historical record indicates their long marriage was a happy one, producing seven children.

Much of what we know of this period in Byzantine history comes from the books written by Constantine VII during the shadowy years he shared the throne with his father-in-law. They include De Ceremoniis, his book of ceremonies; the Vita Basilii, a life of his grandfather, Basil I; and De Administrando Imperio, a book written for his son to use to administer the empire when he took the throne. He was also a painter and art collector. It was during Constantine's lifetime that historians have noted the Byzantines experienced a kind of Renaissance period, no doubt influenced by this unique emperor's patronage.

The Red Fox

Constantinople, November 978

Biting-cold November rain pelted the two soldiers approaching the Great Palace. The icy torrent did little to suppress the high spirits of Manuel Comnenus; his friend's face, though, mirrored the gloomy weather. Comnenus announced their names to the palace's guards with a jaunty air, unfazed by either the downpour or the prospect of being held to account for the recent complicated situation in Nicaea.

Comnenus looked at his second-in-command, Gregory Poulades, clapping a hand on his shoulder. His friend had the twitchy look of a deer catching the scent of a hunter.

"Buck up, soldier. What's the worst that could happen?" he said, trying to encourage Poulades. He shook out his cloak, ignoring the musty smell of damp wool, and handed it to a servant.

"The worst that could happen? Ya mean like being blinded? Or thrown into some dank prison cell? Or sent to the farthest reaches of the empire for the rest of our lives? Did you think I want to live in Cherson for the rest of my life?"

Comnenus shivered in mock horror at the thought of Cherson, a bleak outpost on the far side of the Black Sea, close to the terrifying Pechenegs.

"Cherson? You're right, that would be the worst that could happen. Even worse than being executed." He laughed at his friend's grim expression before pulling him forward down the porticoed corridor leading to the Boukoleon Palace. He would not let Poulades see it, but his own thoughts swung between apprehension and confidence. Military decisions did not always make sense to those not on the battlefield, even if they could be explained.

"You shouldn't laugh. We surrendered Nicaea. They won't be happy 'bout that." Poulades smoothed his damp hair back away from his face, dripping rainwater onto the ground. Their heavy woolen uniforms—the deep red of the Exkoubitores taghmata—clung to their thighs under armor that clattered with every step.

Comnenus forced a nervous smile. "Of course they won't be happy about it. But we made the best of a bad situation. We gave the emperor time to regroup. We lost just a few of our soldiers, and what will Skleros have by the end of winter, eh?"

The reality was Comnenus knew they could end up in Cherson; or they could end up dining with the emperor. The dice were still rolling. He had kept the rebel Bardas Skleros from Constantinople for a couple of crucial months. Perhaps less important to the high and mighty in the palace, he had also saved the local populace from the rebel army. The faces of those people, especially one small child, would have haunted him the rest of his life if he had not.

They approached the reception room where Emperor Basil and his great-uncle, the Parakoimomenos Basil Lecapenos, awaited them. The parakoimomenos had been the one to send Comnenus to Nicaea, lacking any more senior officers. Manuel Comnenus had been second in command of the Exkoubitores, behind its domestic. The domestic had fallen ill with fever, leaving the palace with no alternative to young Comnenus

The assignment to take on the defense of Nicaea had been the opportunity of a lifetime. Now, Comnenus had to answer for his decisions. He had no doubt his actions had best served the emperor. He just needed to get the emperor and parakoimomenos to see it from his point of view.

The two men were led to one of the minor reception rooms in the Boukoleon Palace. Even in this subdued room, the emperor sat on a throne of ebony with armrests plated in gold before a mosaicked wall with Christ Pantocrator looming in fiery Pentecostal red-and-gold glory above him. Emperor Basil, a young man about five years Comnenus's junior, lounged on his throne as he surveyed the two soldiers with hooded eyes and a guarded expression.

The parakoimomenos had a more intimidating aspect. The man was not just the bastard son of Emperor Romanus I, he had served as the leading advisor to five emperors, was more than twice Comnenus's twenty-five years, and was at least a head taller than Comnenus. Also, since his father had had him castrated in early childhood, his voice remained girlish while his words held iron. Altogether, the man presented a disconcerting image.

The parakoimomenos, Basil Lecapenos, wielded the power of the throne on which his great-nephew sat. Even Comnenus's untrained soldier's eye could see the eunuch wore the finest black silk embroidered with gold imperial eagles. The man's imperial red leather boots were embossed with some sort of swirling gold pattern, done at a cost Comnenus could only imagine. A large gold signet ring, inset with onyx, glittered on his right hand. His shoulder-length blond hair shot through with silver had been brushed and oiled to a gleaming sheen. Lecapenos's icy blue eyes glared at the two soldiers daring to report the surrender of such an important city.

Manuel Comnenus and Gregory Poulades made their obeisances before the emperor, who observed them silently. Comnenus took a deep breath and stood relaxed before the dais; the time had passed for worries.

"So you've come to report your abandonment of Nicaea – the city I sent you to defend and hold," the parakoimomenos stopped his diatribe to catch his breath before spitting out more, "and hold it against the rebel Skleros. Can you explain what happened?" he demanded in his high voice.

Comnenus glanced briefly at Poulades. The poor fellow stood to one side, his face red and sweaty with worry. He looked back at the young man on the throne and the older man standing behind it. The emperor's beard was a young man's beard, pale and thin. The parakoimomenos's face was as smooth as a baby's, not a hair to hide the eunuch's anger at losing Nicaea.

"Yes, Excellency, I can." He caught the emperor's eye, a half smile flashing at young Basil for just a moment. The emperor spoke for the first time since Comnenus had entered the room.

"Go ahead. I want to hear what you have to say."

The parakoimomenos scowled, but behind the throne, he was out of the emperor's sight. Manuel Comnenus gave them both a direct look and began his story.

***

Comnenus arrived in Nicaea in late September with about a thousand soldiers of the Exkoubitores taghmata and ten expert siphonatores with their equipment and chemicals for the defense of the city. They arrived a week before Skleros reached the area. The thousand experienced fighters of the taghmata were barely adequate for a city the size of Nicaea, but the contingent of siphonatores and their lethal Greek fire would prove invaluable. The parakoimomenos had been unwilling at first to release the siphonatores and their wicked burning potions, but the importance of Nicaea and Comnenus's persuasive efforts convinced him.

Skleros had been leading his army of six thousand men across Asia Minor toward Constantinople. He needed to capture Nicaea before attempting his assault on the capital. A talented and successful general, he became wealthy during the reign of the young emperor's late uncle and predecessor on the throne, John Tzimiskes. Angered at his demotion under the new regime, Skleros retaliated by attempting to seize the throne from the inexperienced young Basil.

A few days after the imperial army's arrival, scouts sent to watch for Skleros and his men returned with word of their approach. Messages went out to the neighboring villages, and many inhabitants sought the protection of the city's walls.

People soon jammed the city's gates and streets, carting in whatever possessions and foodstuffs they could carry. No one wanted to be in the path of a conquering army— sure to take anything they could find, killing and raping at will. The city's population grew by at least a thousand souls.

Comnenus ran a hand through his red hair, his voice hoarse from shouting instructions. He watched as his soldiers worked to find places for the many people to stay during the siege. Animals grunting and pissing everywhere, voices calling to each other, sweaty bodies competing for space, toppled carts, wailing children—it was the picture of chaos.

In the crush of people, one child caught his eye. A small blond boy was carried by his father, his pregnant mother nearby. The lad, who rested his head on his father's shoulder, looked on in confusion while the father comforted his tearful wife. The child looked straight at Comnenus, his blue eyes fearful at the pandemonium. Comnenus gave the boy a wink and a playful grin. The boy gave a timid smile back before shyly burying his head in his father's shoulder. At least one child would not be crying.

A soldier called down from the ramparts, "Sir, smoke coming from the east."

He scrambled up a ladder to see that Skleros had set a village aflame. Soon others could be seen burning in the distance. People crowded the parapets of the city's walls, crying and groaning over the destruction of their homes and farms in the distance. A pitiable sight, but he had no time for pity. Comnenus ordered the gates shut and everyone but soldiers to leave the walls.

Nicaea's fortifications consisted of a double moat in front of three miles of brick and stone wall, which stood at the height of five men, topped with over one hundred towers spread around three of its sides. The fourth side faced a lake; mole walls stretched out to protect the harbor, a heavy chain slung between their two towers. Skleros would find that way as daunting a challenge as the walls since what boats were not in the harbor had been burned to prevent their use in an assault.

Skleros camped outside the walls the next day. His five thousand men built ladders and siege engines for his attack and scoured the nearby areas for food and forage for their animals. His men took whomever and whatever had stayed outside the city.

Guards stood watch at all hours at the six city gates. The taghmata were not enough to defend the entire city; civilians needed to be armed. The rustic local farmers, angered at the loss of their homes, were not soldiers, but they were strong, eager, and learned fast. Sufficient men had to be assigned to each tower and the walls, no matter where Skleros attacked. Food supplies were assessed. The harvest had suffered from a late hailstorm, so grain supplies stood low, but the farm animals could be slaughtered, and for a time fish could be caught.

Skleros attacked on a bright morning four days later. Hundreds of archers rained down arrows on the soldiers defending Nicaea's walls. Under cover of the arrows, the heavily armored cataphracts and foot soldiers rushed to lean ladders against the walls. The rebels had the rising sun on the eastern horizon at their backs while it half blinded Nicaea's defenders. Their archers could only return fire with difficulty, and Skleros's men took the opportunity to attempt scaling the walls.

Comnenus stood in the tower above the main city gate, sending rapid-fire orders to men along the walls. He was sweating in his armor despite the cooler fall weather. His stomach churned at the sight Skleros's men approaching the walls, ready to climb. He sent Poulades to lead the men on the northern walls, then called to another soldier.

"Maniakes," he said to one of his lieutenants, "see where the ladders are to the south? Get the siphonatores along the walls nearest to them. Once Skleros's men are halfway up one of them, they should start their attack. But make sure our archers are giving them cover; we can't afford to lose even one of them. Understand?"

The soldier nodded and disappeared to relay the instruction.

The siphonatores had a cold, unnerving efficiency about their business. They lobbed the clay pots they had prepared onto the men scrambling up the ladders. Their venomous concoction, secured in the pots, ignited with relentless flames when it broke on impact with a man, a ladder, or the ground. Men spewed with the burning liquid fell screaming to the ground—dying or wishing they were dead. By midday, the attack had subsided.

Poulades appeared at his side to report on the fighting north of the gate. He grimaced at the gruesome howls of their burning attackers while Comnenus surveyed the field.

"I'd feel bad for the poor bastards 'cept I lost two of my best men to their arrows." Poulades held up a handful he'd retrieved from the ground before shoving them into his own quiver to be reused. "One thing's certain—if they keep this up, our archers'll never run out."

"Looks like we have the day," Comnenus said with an exhilarated grin. The rebels scurried to drag their injured or dead comrades from where they lay while Skleros's archers gave cover but could do nothing more. "Skleros had the better position with the sun behind him in the morning. Don't suppose we could induce him to attack in the afternoon," he added drily.

Poulades shrugged at the sight of the receding troops. "No, I don't think so. But just because we have today don't mean there's not a lot of tomorrows." The man's relentless anxiety brought Comnenus the bite of reality he needed.

The acrid stench of sulfur, pine resin, and burning flesh blew through the narrow arrow slit windows of the tower. Comnenus was grateful he knew none of Skleros's men. It would have been worse to do this to men he knew; but they all knew the cost of war.

This first sortie against Nicaea had been a test of the city's ability to defend itself. Next time, Skleros would do better, seeking out any flaw they might have discerned today. But at that moment, looking out over the tiled roofs of Nicaea, Comnenus felt only the euphoria of a battle won.

For the next few days, Skleros's men continued to try scaling the walls, a few making it over before their capture at the guarded points on the walls without siphonatores.

The siphonatores raced between towers, repelling the rebels with their noxious weapons. A few accidents with the clay pots occurred when carelessly handled, spewing their contents onto soldiers before the sand kept ready for such events doused the flames before they spread.

After a week, Skleros gave up on the ladders and brought out the siege engines. Again, the siphonatores proved invaluable. They switched from their clay pots to the long katakorax tubes that sprayed the Greek fire the longer distance to the engines, incinerating them and any who lurked near them. Skleros would have been better off using the wood he built them with for kindling, as it left behind only ashes and splinters.

After about two weeks of fruitless attacks, Skleros realized he could not take the city by force. Instead, he would starve them out with a blockade.

Comnenus soon realized the animals and foodstuffs the farmers who crowded into Nicaea had brought with them would not be enough. Even with strict rationing, with almost nine thousand people to feed, including soldiers, it could not last long.

People grew hungry. Chill autumn winds from the north blew in, and without regular deliveries from woodcutters outside the walls, fuel for heat and cooking grew scarce. Each day, Comnenus circulated throughout the city, trying to bolster the mood while keeping an eye on Skleros from the wall's ramparts.

"How long d'you think we can hold out?" asked Poulades at the end of October, about two weeks into the blockade. The two men strode down a narrow street to the next tower where soldiers stood watch.

Comnenus shook his head. "Not much longer." He glanced at a pile of leaves, blown into a neglected corner against the city wall. The old brown leaves must have been there for some time, dry and crackling and now covered with newly fallen bright red and yellow ones.

"What are we going to do? Will the emperor send an army to relieve us?"

Comnenus had no expectation of that. He had been sent because there were no others available. As he shook his head, the bright leaves on top of the pile sparkling in the sunlight distracted him.

The two men were returning to their quarters when Comnenus noticed an intense discussion going on at the city eparch's office, where rations were being distributed. A thin man held a small blond boy as he begged for more food.

"My wife has just given birth. Don't you understand, she can't come for her share and she needs food for herself and the child," the man said

"Rules is rules. Everyone has to come for they's share. No exceptions," said the gruff official. He turned to the next supplicant, ignoring the man's pleading.

The small boy was thinner than he remembered, but Comnenus recognized the child he had seen the day Skleros had camped outside the city walls, burning the surrounding villages. The rationing had left him listless, although he glanced briefly at Comnenus, smiling halfheartedly.

"Soldier," Comnenus said to the official divvying up the foodstuffs.

The man glanced up at him briefly, and then went to attention. "Sir, what's it I can do for you?"

He gestured to the man with the boy. "You can make sure this man has food for his wife, who just had a baby."

"But, sir, if I—" the soldier began.

"Soldier," Comnenus growled at the underling. "Do you really expect a woman who's just given birth to crawl to your desk? Give the man her portion."

"No, sir. Yes, sir," he agreed with some reluctance.

The man with the boy looked at the city's commanding officer, confused at the unexpected intercession. Comnenus tousled the child's hair as the father thanked him.

***

Comnenus brooded over his choices as he tried to sleep that night. They could wait for the emperor to send troops to relieve them. Not likely. They could stay and slowly starve to death. Most likely, as things stood, but not good.

There had to be another way. Comnenus thought back to the lad he had seen in his father's arms and the pregnant mother. They reminded him of his own parents and the terrible time when war had driven them from their home with small children, his mother pregnant with him. His mother would never speak of that rough time, and it was a faded memory for his brothers. But there was that day he and his father had been alone at dinner and his father had told the story of fleeing in the night, fearful of the Bulgarian army passing close, without food for days. It was a small shadow on an otherwise untroubled childhood. That small boy and his parents reminded him of his own family then.

Crickets chirped outside, and his mind drifted into happier childhood memories, recalling the trouble he had gotten into as a boy—always playing tricks on his mother and brothers. He chuckled at the thought of how riled he could get his brothers and how he somehow managed to be some distance away when that anger erupted. They had called him "the Red Fox" in those days.

Thoughts of the city's troubles returned. His soldiers needed to get out of the city, and so did the people. Boats moored in the harbor could do it, but there were not enough for nine thousand of them, and they wouldn't get far with Skleros's archers out along the lake's perimeter beyond the mole walls.

Restless in the stifling air, Comnenus rose from his bed in frustration. He opened a shutter to let in fresh air. A handful of leaves blew through the window, some dried to brown, some still bright gold, spinning and tumbling in the moonlight. He looked down at the leaves, tired and confused, before returning to bed. Wrapping himself in his blanket, he fell into deep sleep.

***

Comnenus opened his eyes at first light, alert and with every nerve in his body tingling. He knew now what he would have to do. It would be the biggest trick he ever played, but he knew it would work. He had not felt this sure of anything since they had arrived in Nicaea. He rose from his bed and went to the door.

"Gregory," he called out. "I need carts full of sand tonight."

He spent that day arranging for the carts and sand to be delivered to the warehouses under cover of night. Gregory Poulades had looked skeptical when his senior officer explained his scheme.

"Skleros is not some kid. He's been around and is not easily fooled," he said.

Comnenus shrugged and grinned. "So he's cocky. Thinks he knows all the tricks. Might make it easier." He had fooled his own brothers many times, and they should have known better, too.

Two days later, the trap was ready to be set with the bait. Comnenus sent for a couple of prisoners taken when Skleros had tried to come over the walls. The men approached him warily, chains still on their wrists. One wore the insignia of Stratore, the commander of a fifty-man unit, while the other was a more junior officer. Comnenus made sure the door was closed, sat down with them, and poured wine into three cups. Warm loaves of bread on a platter and bowls of olives sat next to the jug. Now came the tricky part.

He gave them an embarrassed smile before speaking.

"I'm really sorry to have kept you in chains these past weeks. I hope you haven't been treated badly."

The men glanced at each other over the rims of their cups as they drained them, looking perplexed at the unexpected solicitude.

"We're well enough," said the stratore, a few gray hairs threading his beard. He put his cup down, his chains rattling as he did so.

"Ah, I'm glad to hear that. And you, my friend," Comnenus said to the younger officer, a brawny man with dark hair making short work of one of the loaves, "have you been getting enough to eat? You look like you have a healthy appetite. We've got plenty of food if you'd like more. I reckon the city can hold out maybe two years with what's in the city's warehouses."

Comnenus smiled, showing two mostly straight rows of teeth.

"Well, maybe a bit more would not go amiss," said the young man through a mouthful, venturing a smile back at his captor.

"Of course, of course, I'll take care of it today." Comnenus took his own cup of wine and drank it down with gusto. "Even if we fight on different sides of Nicaea's walls, it doesn't mean we are truly enemies." He refilled the three cups.

"How's you mean? We fight for Skleros; you fight for the emperor," said the older man, raising a questioning eyebrow.

Comnenus snorted. "Just because I fight for the emperor doesn't mean I'm his man. My ma's family came from Skleros lands; that's where my loyalty is. But the emperor and that uncle of his have my younger brother under lock and key at the palace. They said he would be their 'guest' while I am fighting, but we know better, don't we?" he said with a disgusted frown.

The older man shook his head as he popped an olive into his mouth. "Bad luck for you." A moment later, he spit the pit onto the floor.

The younger man nodded agreement. "Too bad you couldn't jump over to our side."

Comnenus sighed and gave a small shrug. "I could never abandon George; he's my only brother. I've thought over and over about how to get out of here, find some way to get him out of the palace, and join up with Skleros, but there doesn't seem to be any way to do it."

He poured more wine into empty cups.

The older man had a sentimental look on his face. "Had a younger brother named George meself. We was always fighting, but anyone try coming 'tween us, they got the worst of it. He died fighting the Persians, maybe ten years back." He tore off a corner of bread and began to chew.

"So you know how I feel," said Comnenus in an appropriately somber voice.

"That I do, sir, that I do."

The conversation lapsed as the three men sipped their wine in contemplative silence.

Comnenus slapped his cup onto the table, startling his two chained companions.

"I'm so glad we had this conversation. Talking with you has made me realize I can't continue this way. I have to find a way to get my brother free and join General Skleros. I can't spend my life fighting for that prancing eunuch and the green child he's put on the throne."

The older man belched softly and frowned. "Not sure how's to be done."

"I think I've an idea that might work. Tell me what you think. How about if I let the two of you return to Skleros and you tell him I'm willing to leave Nicaea with my men—just let him have it—if he lets us leave undisturbed. Then, once I'm back in Constantinople, I'll get George free from the palace and be back here, reporting to General Skleros."

"Won't the emperor wonder why you gave the city over?" the younger officer asked skeptically.

"You're right. He will ask. Maybe my plan won't work." Comnenus, deflated, put his head in his hands and bent over, elbows on the table, the problem defeating him.

"How's 'bout you tell him the city ran out of victuals? By the time truth comes out, you'll have George and be gone," the younger man suggested helpfully.

"That's right," said the older man. "And you'll do General Skleros a good turn, too. He's got men to feed, and he'll be glad of the grain you've got stored. Once you're back, he'll be sure to show his gratitude."

Comnenus was elated at the suggestion. The conversation could not have gone better.

"I wish I'd known you two all my life. That's a brilliant idea," said the man known as the Red Fox in childhood. "But the general will have to let me and my men leave in peace and, of course, anyone in the city who wants to go with us. Otherwise, the emperor will figure out my trick. D'you think Skleros'd be willing?"

The two soldiers nodded in earnest.

"You send us out to him, and we'll be sure he gets the word. You'll have your George afore Advent comes."

Comnenus sat before the two men, brow furrowed, seeming to give their words grave consideration. Then he shook his head.

"Can't do it. Too chancy. S'pose Skleros doesn't believe you? S'pose his army slaughters us on the way out? My friends, I can't take the risk. Better to sit here for the next two years until the food runs out."

The two men protested, seeing their chance of freedom slipping away. "No indeed, sir. We'll vouch for you."

"No, I can't. He won't believe you." Comnenus looked crestfallen. "My men trust me. I can't risk their lives."

"I know," said the younger soldier. "You send us back to the general with a few sacks of grain. It'll show him you have food to last years. And he'll be glad to pull a trick on that eunuch in the palace. He can't stand the bastard."

The grizzled stratore scratched the side of his face, considering his subordinate's suggestion, before giving a nod of agreement.

"He does hate the fellow, makes no secret of it. General'd be happy to pull one over on him."

Comnenus painted a dubious look on his face before seeming to come around reluctantly. "I guess we can try it; see what happens."

The two men relaxed, looking pleased at their ability to persuade this erstwhile enemy. Comnenus almost felt sorry for them, knowing this trick would end any hopes they might have of promotions.

Within a few minutes, the two men were unchained and out in the city's narrow winding streets, following Comnenus on a circuitous path to the grain warehouses.

"I don't want to arouse any suspicion, so we'll go to three different warehouses and get a sack from each," he confided to them.

The men waited outside while Comnenus retrieved the sacks. Even from the outside of each warehouse, their eyes bulged at the sight of the large wooden bins filled to the brim with tawny grain.

Comnenus clapped a hand on each of the men's shoulders at the city's main gate.

"Be sure to tell the general everything I told you. He can signal for a parley, and I'll come out to make it official. If he agrees, of course." Comnenus looked apprehensive.

"Not to worry, sir. He'll agree," said the younger man, full of the wineskin's confidence.

Comnenus nodded and closed the gate behind the two burdened men. He stared at its heavy oak beams with an excited gleam in his eyes.

Poulades stepped out of the shadows where he had watched this part of the performance, shaking his head. "They seem convinced."

One side of Comnenus's mouth twisted up as he glanced at Poulades.

"I think so, too, but we'll know better tomorrow."

***

At sunrise, a message arrived for Comnenus asking him to meet with Skleros in the field between the camp and the city walls. A cold rain drizzled when the two men rode out for their meeting.

The general, a burly man in his mid-forties, wore a heavy cloak over his polished armor. He gave a curt nod at his opponent, sizing him up. Comnenus saluted, pasting an anxious look on his face.

"My men tell me you have family from my lands." Comnenus knew Skleros had to first ascertain whether he really had any connections.

"Yes, my mother's family was Erotikos. Perhaps you've heard of my uncle Isaac? He sponsored me when I joined the Exkoubitores. We were close," he said, mentioning the only relative he knew from that side of his family, who was fortunately deceased.

"Ah, yes. Isaac Erotikos was a good man," Skleros said with the air of a man who barely recalled the avuncular Isaac. He pondered Comnenus for a moment, the leather creaking as he shifted in his saddle. "How is it your brother found himself as a guest in the palace?"

"We've no other family left but each other. My parents wanted him to enter the Church, and he's only fifteen, so I got him into the Hagia Sophia's school. That cursed eunuch has spies everywhere; George was snatched away to the palace even before I knew I'd be sent here." No harm in spreading the aroma of incense around.

Skleros chewed on the side of his mouth, thinking. "How much food is left in Nicaea?"

"I reckon we have enough to last through a siege for two years. Your men saw our grain bins yesterday."

Skleros squinted at him, weighing his choices.

"So you want to leave the city to me, with warehouses full to bursting, so you can extricate your brother from the bastard's claws. And then you'll return to fight for me?"

Comnenus's voice cracked with a soft, desperate moan. "It has to. I need to get him away from the palace. I just need a little help from you."

Skleros's brow furrowed at this show of emotion before coming to a decision.

"You, your men, and whoever wants to go with you can leave tomorrow at first light. Take only what you can carry; I don't want a city stripped of provisions. Once

your brother is free, be back here with him.
I'll have a place for you both."

Comnenus's face broke into a relieved
smile.

"Yes, General. You can be sure I'll be
back as soon as I have him. Thank you."

The two men parted as the rain grew
heavier, both eager to reach shelter. Comnenus would not look at Poulades until he
stood with the city's gates shut behind him.
Then he dismounted and leaned against the
rough stone city walls, laughing exultantly.

Poulades stared at his commander, in-
credulous at what he had just seen.

"You have balls made of iron."

Comnenus wiped the tears of laughter
from his eyes. "Did I ever tell you I grew up
with three older brothers? I pulled tricks like
this on them all the time. I haven't had this
much fun since my brothers fell for them."

"Hmm. It's a miracle you survived." Poulades looked around the street leading from
the gate. Only a few forlorn souls had ventured out in the cold rain. "I guess I need to
get word out to leave tomorrow." Poulades
pulled up the hood of his cloak and started
toward the barracks, shaking his head in
amazement.

***

The first gray light of day saw the streets of Nicaea thronged with soldiers and the multitudes seeking to leave before Skleros's men arrived. Poulades and a few men were doing their best to keep order among the confused and frightened civilians while Comnenus made sure the fighting men would be ready should Skleros turn the game around.

He was shouting orders to the siphonatores when he noticed the young family he'd seen that day in September when the rebel army arrived. The small blond boy was yawning in his father's arms while the young mother, holding a tiny bundle close, looked exhausted. Still weakened from childbirth, she would not have the stamina to walk as the others would.

He whistled over to Poulades. "We need a cart for the women with babies." Poulades gave his commander a harried look and nodded.

"And one for the old and sick," Comnenus added, noting several stooped elderly people walking with their canes.

Poulades sent a few soldiers looking for mules and carts, and within an hour, the exodus from Nicaea began.

The road out of the city was blessedly paved for about a mile, relieving the procession of the need to slog through mud. On either side of it, Skleros's army stood watching them, his men calling to the imperial soldiers to join them. Comnenus's men made the same invitation back.

Comnenus rode at the front of the cavalcade, his face a mask of defeated military formality. The victorious Skleros, wearing a black leather corselet embossed with gold eagles, watched the departure from astride an armored gray stallion. The animal snorted and pawed at the ground in the morning mist. Comnenus saluted respectfully to the triumphant general and nodded to his two recent prisoners, who stood close by Skleros, looking pleased with themselves.

As they passed General Skleros, a few of the emperor's soldiers were heard loudly grumbling about why they were abandoning the city when it was so amply provisioned. Comnenus looked back in time to see Skleros give a nod of satisfaction on hearing those complaints. The procession out of Nicaea went on until mid-morning before finally passing out of the rebel army's sight.

***

Poulades spurred his horse forward to join Comnenus when they reached the unpaved road. Already some of the braver civilians had begun peeling off to return to their homes—or what was left of them.

"How long before Skleros realizes what you've done?" he asked.

Comnenus peered at him, the side of his mouth twisting up while he considered. "Maybe a day or two, if we're lucky. Unless those two soldiers have the instincts of a hunting dog, it'll take them that long to find the warehouses. I'm not sure I could find them again myself after the labyrinthine path I took them on. So we'll have a decent head start."

Poulades still looked anxious. "Aren't you worried about the palace? They expected us to hold Nicaea."

"That's what they said. But what they really wanted was to stop Skleros from reaching Constantinople. We held him for over a month, past the end of the fighting season, and now all he has is an empty shell of a city. Won't do him much good. And the whole of the empire will be laughing at him. What could be better?"

Poulades shook his head. "Hope you're right. If ya aren't, we may need to look for another profession."

***

Manuel Comnenus stopped speaking, interrupted by servants lighting lamps as sunset approached.

"So what did you show those soldiers?" asked the emperor.

"The usual grain bins. But I had them mostly filled with sand, then we covered the top of them with a little grain to make it look like we had plenty. I didn't let them get too close."

The emperor and the parakoimomenos glanced at each other, their mouths twisting up before breaking into hilarious laughter. Comnenus thought he would never get used to the sound of the eunuch's girlish guffawing, but had the wisdom to keep his face blank.

"No one will want to join Skleros now that he's been made a fool of," the parakoimomenos said.

The emperor grinned at the two men.

"You've done me and the empire a great service, and I'm grateful. You must join me at dinner this evening and tell me more about the siege. I wish I'd been there."

"We'd be happy to join you," said Comnenus.

"Oh, and bring that famous younger brother, George, too," said the emperor in afterthought.

Comnenus's eyes sparkled playfully before he confessed, "Sire, that would be impossible. You see, I have no younger brother."

Author's Note:

Emperor Basil II reigned for almost fifty years and became one of the most militarily successful Byzantine emperors. The elder of the two grandsons of Constantine Porphyrogenitus and his wife, Helena Lecapena, he left the empire with strong borders and a full treasury. His one great weakness was a lack of good, or even any, succession planning, and he was followed by a string of greedy and/or incompetent rulers.

The years of weak rulers were briefly interrupted when the oldest son of this story's Manuel Comnenus, Isaac Comnenus, took the throne in 1061 for two years before abdicating due to ill health. The trend of bad rulers continued almost unbroken for another eighteen years until the child of Manuel's younger son, John, his grandson, Alexios Comnenus, took the throne in 1081, leading the empire to a hard fought recovery. With the exception of the fifty-three years of Latin rule following the Fourth Crusade, every Byzantine emperor until its fall in 1453 could claim descent from this family.

The high point of Bardas Skleros's revolt was probably just before he entered Nicaea to discover its sand-filled grain bins. The emperor's forces defeated him a few months after this story, and he fled to an uncomfortable exile in Persia.

Basil Lecapenos, the parakoimomenos, was the illegitimate youngest child of Emperor Romanus I. His father had him castrated as an infant, presumably so he would be able to have a position within the palace. I suspect Romanus also wanted to keep the throne for his legitimate descendants. This talented and capable man held the position of leading advisor to five emperors: his brother-in-law Constantine VII Porphyrogenitus, nephew Romanus II, Nicephoros II Phocas, John I Tzimiskes, and finally to his great-nephew Basil II. His proximity to the throne gave him access to the treasury, and he amassed great wealth, which ultimately brought about his downfall. Basil II's abstemious habits led him to take an increasingly dim view of his great-uncle's lavish lifestyle. Seven years after this story, the parakoimomenos was stripped of his office, had his lands and wealth confiscated, and was exiled, dying soon afterward.

Alexiad

"You are certain he has agreed to our plan? This is so important," Dowager Empress Irene said urgently. Anna Comnena felt her mother's sharp gray eyes probing her face for any qualms or sign of hesitation. The older woman kept an iron grip on Anna's elbow as they walked apace through the garden on Anna's estate overlooking the Bosphorus on that cool morning. Irene of-

ten goaded her daughter on, reminding Anna of her humiliation at being denied the
throne. So much for both of them depended
on the success of their revolt.

"Yes, Mama, I am certain. He agreed to it
last night. He's my husband; I trust him. He
left early this morning to begin recruiting
others who will support us—Isaac Kontostephanos, Nicholas Taronites, and others
unhappy with my brother," came Anna's
too-quick response. She feared not meeting
her mother's ideals for an imperial princess.
It was easier to do as her mother wished
than risk being frozen out. Easier, too, not
to mention her husband's reluctance when
they had spoken the night before.

Her husband knew better than most of
Anna's indignation at being passed over by
the father she adored after the promise of
the throne made in her early years. Even so,
he had been shocked when she disclosed the
scheme for them to seize the crown. He
clearly doubted Anna would have dreamed
this up on her own; not after her brother
had taken the throne so smoothly after
Alexios's death eight months earlier. He accused Irene of conjuring it, and at first
wanted no part. He had given his grudging

agreement after a long argument and a torrent of tears convinced him of her determination to seize her birthright.

Irene may have conceived this plan for her own reasons, but it was balm to Anna's injured pride.

Anna understood why Irene hungered for power such as her formidable mother-in-law had once wielded through Alexios. Emperor Alexios Comnenus had never allowed Irene to govern, even during his months on campaign. Yet he had allowed his own mother to rule as regent in his absence during his early years on the throne. His lack of confidence in his wife had humiliated Irene. She was even more superfluous at her son's court since Alexios's death. Her son treated her with respect, but he, too, excluded her from any authority. Irene's approval, however, was more important to Anna.

"Look, here he is now," Anna said as she saw her husband enter the garden from a door in their house. Her smile faded in confusion at the sight of him. His pale face looked unhappy and his eyes evasive. At first, she could not discern the other man in the shadows who followed her husband.

The man came into the light, and she realized who it was.

"Dear God. John is with him," she murmured as her mother's grip slackened. John Axouch, her brother's best friend and most loyal ally. He was dressed in full military regalia, sword at his side.

Her knees almost buckled. The shock made her heart thump painfully and she felt chilled, as though all her blood had seeped out of her body.

John nodded at Anna's husband, who shrank against the far wall. A sturdy man with the black beard and swarthy skin of his Turkish ancestors, John strode over to where Anna and Irene stood, transfixed at his appearance. He bowed deeply to them before speaking.

"Your Grace, Lady Anna." John glanced first at the dowager empress before studying Anna at greater length. Irene glared at him with her usual contempt. Alexios had given him to her to foster when John was five, but she had never taken to this child of the heathens.

Anna drew herself up under his baleful gaze, trying to maintain imperial dignity. This soldier had often been assigned as her escort when Anna and her mother had joined Alexios on campaign in the years before his death. The camaraderie of those years had held the hint of deeper affections, at least on John's part. Now, though, the warm eyes she recalled had turned to a stony hardness. After several moments with tension as alive as a hissing snake coiled between them, he spoke.

"Lady Anna, your husband confessed to the plot you and your mother conceived to remove your brother from the imperial throne so that you and he would rule together. Do you deny this treason?"

Before Anna could speak, her mother blurted out, "It was Anna's idea. I had no part in it. I tried to convince her not to go ahead with it."

Irene had let go of Anna's arm and put space between them when John appeared. Anna looked at her mother, dumbfounded at this accusation, her fair skin flushing at her mother's betrayal. Irene's calculating eyes warned her dutiful daughter not to give her away.

John Axouch saw this brief soundless exchange between mother and daughter and sighed. Anna knew his many years in close quarters with her family left him with few surprises about Irene. Still, she gave him a defensive look for her mother's sake. He returned the look with a skeptical frown before speaking again, his voice stern.

"The emperor, always benevolent and forgiving, has decided that rather than have his beloved mother and sister executed for this crime, as is his right, you will both enter the Kecharitomene Monastery. There you will live out the remainder of your lives."

Anna sat down on a nearby bench, stunned, eyes wide with shock, hands clutched at her throat. How many heartbeats had passed from when she had been betrayed, first by her husband and then by her mother? Irene stood motionless with an odd, sour smile frozen on her face. Anna shot an accusatory look at her husband, skulking in the garden corner, somehow more disappointed in him than her mother. He returned it with his own silent accusation, looking disgusted at the women's recklessness.

"I can't leave. What of my children?" Anna cried, her face in her hands, trying to control the nausea sweeping over her. Her youngest was only nine years old.

"They'll remain here with your husband. The emperor has given his permission for them to visit you at Kecharitomene," said John. His voice sounded gruff, but no honeyed tone could sweeten that news.

John frowned at the two foolish women, one almost turned to stone before him and the other weeping. Anna felt ill when she realized there would be no delay. He turned back toward the lovely villa and raised a hand, signaling the appearance of a half dozen Varangians. The blond soldiers in their red court uniforms carelessly trampled on her rosebushes as they escorted Anna Comnena and the Dowager Empress Irene Ducaena away. Her heart almost broke when she saw the pale faces of her children, the youngest crying, as they stared from the villa's windows.

Anna called out to her husband as he followed the soldiers, "How could you do this? You could have been emperor."

He just shook his head.

***

Constantinople, December 1, 1137

Most days, she refused to think of all she had lost that terrible spring day eighteen years before. But this day, her birthday, the anger rose to a boil, her fists clenched at the injustice of it. The waste of her life, so much of it entombed in these brick walls, left her seething.

Anna Comnena paced through the monastery garden while the events of that long past April day replayed in her head. Pebbles crunched under her rapid footsteps and crowded out the sound of the Sunday hymns the nuns sang in the nearby church. Her mother, Empress Irene, had founded this place, the Kecharitomene Monastery, more than a quarter century earlier. The name meant "full of grace." Anna snorted at the thought of finding any grace in what was now her prison.

A frigid north wind blew gray clouds into the imperial city of Constantinople. The sky darkened with threatening snow, coming early this first day of December. She remembered well her mother's stories of the joy and celebrations held fifty-five years earlier at her birth. Anna had been their first child, the "born in the purple room" princess of her father, the new Emperor Alexios, and the city had rejoiced. Now, she was a dusty, forgotten relic. Her own daughters were now dead or distant, and her sons, embarrassed at her continued existence, were serving her accursed brother John, the one who called himself emperor. She expected no warm solicitations from her children. The monastery's superior, the Hegoumena Maria, might acknowledge her at the midday meal. Anna would almost rather be ignored than to have to respond with courtesy to such feigned consideration.

Her mind slipped back to that day eighteen years before that had seen the start of her first incarceration, and she shivered at the memory. Anna pulled the fox fur mantle closer against the wind, the garment a plush remnant of her golden days as an imperial princess. Suddenly weary, she sat on one of the garden's weathered benches and frowned in contemplation of the stunted rosebush before her. Years earlier, when first incarcerated, Anna and her mother had planted everything in this garden to occupy their time—roses, poppies, herbs, and even a few fruit trees at the far end. Her mother had told her not to plant this rosebush in a spot shaded for the best part of the day. The small bush had ceased growing and only bloomed on occasion, although it had survived.

Anna spent seven years with her mother in these walls until Irene's death. Her husband then pleaded with her brother for her release, to return to their home and his bed, arguing he would prevent her from involvement in any other conspiracy. A ghostly sort of existence as few sought an association with her, but she could come and go and converse as she pleased. She had had ten years outside these walls, though as a disgraced and defeated rebel before her recent return following her husband's death.

Anna could not help but imagine how different their lives would have been if their rebellion had succeeded. Her husband had disappointed her with his weak concern for honor. He should have understood how she felt—to be raised until she was eleven to think she would be empress, and then to have it snatched away. She always felt as though people laughed at her for it. He said he never heard such laughter, but the smirks and whispering she saw stung her.

"I swore an oath of loyalty to your brother, as your own father asked on his deathbed. You know he loved you, but no man prefers a daughter to succeed him rather than a son. I never, never desired the throne, yet you and your mother plotted behind my back," he had said to her in anger during a visit with their children in those first years spent here with her mother. "You did this to us."

Her father's preference for her brother to succeed him still grated. She had tried so much to impress him with her erudition, her charitable works, even playing chess with him—a game she could not figure out well enough to defeat her father often.

She had received a terse note from her brother after her husband's death over a year earlier. "My condolences on the loss of your husband. He was a great friend to me, and I will mourn his death. I expect you will now retire to our mother's rooms at Kecharitomene." That was the end of it. As a princess, she would not beg for anything—even her freedom—from her brother.

Now, back inside the monastery's walls, the deep note from the striking of the semantron again ordered her silent, unvarying days.

Anna glanced up at the few seagulls wheeling in the lowering sky, screeching at each other. She smelled the sharp tang of smoke curling through the air as fires were lit in the city to chase the chill away. The street noises of shopkeepers and children outside the monastery's high walls faded as residents hurried home. A few flakes swirled through air that was as cold as a eunuch's bed. Still, returning to the confinement of the two rooms she shared with a serving girl, with its warm braziers, held no appeal.

Here in the city of Constantinople, the greatest and most populous city in the world, she might as well have been sitting in the desert for all the company Anna now had. The rules her mother instituted for the monastery at its founding meant little conversation and fewer visitors. For Anna, educated in mathematics and rhetoric, history and medicine, this was a dull existence. She had traveled throughout the empire with her parents and had been the patroness of a hospital in the city. As a princess, she had sponsored scholars and entertained learned men. Anna missed the sparkling conversations of those men of learning, even if they had scattered like a flock of birds into which an arrow has been shot following her arrest.

In honest retrospect, Anna felt sick at the cost of her foolhardy attempt to overthrow her brother. He had campaigned with the empire's generals—their father, uncles, and cousins. He had known how to gain the support of those men of power. She and her mother had not.

Snowflakes fell like frozen tears on her face. She swept them away. She wished Irene had explained or apologized for her denial to John Axouch of her involvement in the plot. They had spent seven years together within these walls, but her mother never spoke of it. Anna, ever the dutiful child, did whatever her mother asked, treating her with the utmost respect, even after that day. She somehow dreaded confronting her mother, which might have revealed her mother's uglier side. Irene lay entombed beside Alexios these past eleven years. Anna could now admit—to herself, if no one else—that her mother had not been a wise or loving woman. That bitter lesson came too late.

Anna stretched out her foot, clad in its faded imperial red leather boot, rustling the stiff grass underneath. She felt veiled and forgotten in the garden as snow began to fall in earnest. Her blue eyes peered into the sky, now barren since the birds had all flown to their nests. She pushed back a loose strand of hair, faded to russet from the vibrant scarlet she had once shared with her father, and pursed her lips. The young Sister Irene saw her from the portico and approached, her black novice's habit soon speckled with snow. Anna stiffened at the thought of the girl's relentless cheerfulness. She resolved to maintain the diffidence of an imperial princess born in the purple room.

"Lady Anna, Hegoumena Maria has asked that you join us in the refectory for our meal. She says it is your birthday and wants to offer special prayers on the occasion," the bright-eyed nun said as she sat beside Anna without invitation.

Anna raised an eyebrow at this familiarity but said only, "Thank you, Sister. You may tell the Hegoumena I will join her shortly." Then, bitterly to herself, "So little like the old days."

"The old days, Lady Anna? What do you mean?"

She wished this child would just leave her alone. Had she forgotten her vow of silence so quickly?

Anna spoke sharply, impatient at Sister Irene's ignorance, "Yes, the old days. When I was young and my father, Emperor Alexios, ruled, my birthday was a great celebration. I was his firstborn child, betrothed to Constantine Ducas, the son of an emperor. We were to reign with my father."

Anna did not think of Constantine often anymore. Her golden-haired first betrothed, as handsome as his mother had been beautiful—until he had begun coughing blood and her parents had ended the betrothal. She had mourned his death some months later, even though by then she had been betrothed to the man who would be her husband.

"Your father was Emperor Alexios?" the little nun asked, astonished. "He died long before I was born. What was he like?"

Anna's eyebrows rose in surprise at the child's ignorance of both her and her father. "You have not been told of him?" she asked, surprised at the girl's ignorance of her illustrious father. Most girls were barely taught how to read, but she should have known of her father's glorious reign and her own imperial dignity.

"Not so much, Lady Anna." The girl's wide brown eyes regarded her with curiosity. The snow fell faster now, covering all with a thin white sheet.

"A terrible omission in your education," Anna said brusquely, shaking the snow off her gloved hands, scowling as she did so. "He led great armies against the empire's enemies, winning victories and the respect of his adversaries. His wisdom and justice in ruling were renowned. I will have to tell you more of him someday," she said, although she had no such intention. She stood and stretched, wrapping the fur cloak closer. "But now I must ready myself for dinner," and she turned to stride to her rooms, a blur amongst the spinning flakes.

***

In the morning, after matins, Anna joined the nuns in the refectory to stitch garments for the poor—the Sisters' daily task. She had little else to occupy her at that time of year. Most of the two dozen nuns living in the monastery were gathered in the room, the rest set on tasks elsewhere on their grounds. Anna took up her needle in glum silence with the others, except for Sister Irene, whose turn it was that day to read aloud from the Bible for the edification of the other sisters as they worked.

Anna's face took on a pinched expression at the sight of the novice sitting in the reader's chair. The dreary monotony of daily needlework was dull enough. The princess felt ready to scream at the thought of adding Sister Irene's barely coherent reading to the day's tedium. Hegoumena Maria had taken to sitting nearby when Sister Irene read to coach the girl when she stumbled, but her efforts had so far been futile.

It being the season of Christ's nativity, the chosen readings were from Isaiah and full of names Sister Irene's tongue blundered over. Zebulon became Zebon while Naphtali emerged somehow as Phalanti. The hegoumena's whispered corrections only accentuated the novice's errors. Anna and several of the less patient nuns rolled their eyes in annoyance at the girl's attempts.

Afterward, the women prepared to return for midday prayers in the church. Anna felt uneasy, though, when she noticed the hegoumena looking at her the way her father's hawks had eyed their prey.

Later, Anna received a summons from Hegoumena Maria. She arrived in the superior's office, apprehensive after recalling the look she had noticed from the nun that morning.

"Lady Anna, I am sure you have noticed Sister Irene's poor readings during refectory," the older woman said, looking at Anna through narrowed eyes.

"Yes, Hegoumena. But the child is young. She may not have had good teachers before coming here," Anna agreed, wary at this unexpected discussion of a girl who was as humble as a wooden spoon.

"Yes, well, that is apparent," the hegoumena said drily. "And it is for that reason I would like you to take on the task of tutoring her at reading and writing. Of course, I will release her from her obligation of silence during those lessons."

Anna sat stunned at this indignity. She finally sputtered out a response. "Hegoumena, I am an imperial princess, not a tutor. I think one of the other nuns would be better suited to such a task." She enunciated each word through clenched teeth to emphasize the outrageous nature of this proposal.

"Yes, you are an imperial princess," the hegoumena conceded cheerfully. "But the other nuns live under the rule of silence, as your mother required when she established Kecharitomene, and I would rather not release more than one from her vows—too many opportunities for frivolous gossip. While you live amongst us, however, you have not taken such a vow and may speak as you wish. So I think you would be best."

Anna pursed her lips in silent irritation at her mother's strictures; many monasteries did not have that limitation. Why had her mother insisted on it? She glanced around the room, searching for some escape. A last, a desperate suggestion to avoid such a degrading task occurred to her. "Would it not be possible to hire a tutor from outside to teach Sister Irene?"

"Lady Anna, again, your mother's rules permit only limited visits from outsiders, so the peace of our home is not disturbed. I believe Sister Irene will need more than a few lessons." The older woman's smile held both encouragement and unbending resolve. "Really, I think you would be best."

Anna had played enough chess to recognize checkmate. She swallowed this new humiliation with difficulty before answering the gray-haired nun fingering her prayer beads.

"When do you want us to begin?"

The victor's smile broadened. "In the morning, after third-hour prayer. I think an hour each morning for at least a month. Then we shall see how she progresses."

***

The next day, shy Sister Irene joined Anna in her rooms for their first lesson. The little nun glanced around in awe of her tutor's rich accommodations—the four charcoal-filled braziers burning red, thick rugs, cushions, silk curtains, and windows covered in glass that kept out the north wind through the winter but let in the light. Anna and her serving girl had earlier arranged a table so tutor and student could sit next to each other.

The girl took her seat in the proffered chair. She bent her head and peered down at her hands folded in her lap, too timid to look up. The dark-haired novice had entered the monastery six months earlier and looked about fifteen, younger than most of Anna's grandchildren. Next to the young nun, Anna drummed her fingers in irritation at the idea she should be teaching this nobody. But the sooner begun, the sooner done. She started with an inquiry into the education the girl had received thus far.

"Sister, how long did you receive tutoring in grammar?"

The nun looked up at her, surprised. "I had no tutoring, Lady Anna."

"Well, surely you had a tutor. You know how to read a little," Anna responded with a frown, her voice sharp.

"No, Lady, I had no tutoring," she protested. "My father only had the money to educate my brothers; we girls learned what we could from them."

Anna's frown softened, recalling her own pleas to be educated more than other girls. But her parents had been able to pay for her tutors, and they were the best ones available.

"What of your mother? Did she not try to teach you?" Anna asked. Irene must have received some instruction.

"I was my mother's last child. There were seven older than me, so she had little time for it. Mama died when I was six." Irene stopped speaking for a moment, wiping away a tear.

"My father did his best for us," she continued. "My brothers have positions in the army, and my two sisters had dowries to marry. But by then, there was no money left for me. When my father learned that Kecharitomene did not require a gift when a novice entered, he applied for me. And since our family is related to the Kekaumenos family, I was accepted."

Anna felt her irritation for the girl's ignorance melting away. The girl had had few opportunities as the poor relation of a waning noble family. If Sister Irene's father had died before she entered the monastery, she might have ended up in a brothel, or worse. With more patience, Anna placed her grandmother's old psalter in front of Irene. It seemed as good a place to start as any. They began to read together King David's psalms.

***

Sister Irene improved steadily through the winter months. After the first month, when

Sister Irene's turn in refectory came again, her reading needed only a little assistance from the hegoumena. Despite her initial resentment at being assigned such a task, Anna took real pleasure in her student's progress and promised Hegoumena Maria that Sister Irene would be even better with further tutelage. So the superior allowed their meetings to continue.

One morning in March, after an especially difficult passage from the Book of the Apocalypse, Sister Irene asked, "When you were tutored as a child, were you also taught from the Bible?" gesturing at the holy book on Anna's table.

"I was for some of it. But I asked for other books as well. I read histories, philosophy, poetry, and plays, and I learned mathematics. My parents thought Aristotle would ruin me, but I promised he would not," Anna said, smiling as she recalled her pleasure at winning their approval for teachers.

"What were your parents like?" Irene asked.

Anna smiled in fond reminiscence of her indulged childhood before speaking.

"My father was not a tall man, not like the big Varangian guards, but no one doubted he commanded and ruled the empire. Even those barbarian Franks could see that when they came through to fight in the Holy Land. My mother was devoted to my father, doing all she could to see to his comfort. They had nine children, but only three of us still live."

The little nun's face melted in sympathy before she spoke again.

"On your birthday, you told me in the rose garden that your father had been a great general, respected by all. When were his battles?"

This question made Anna pause, her eyebrows drawn close. Her father had spent the first fifteen years of his reign fighting on all sides of the empire. After he defeated one enemy, others burst out like moles digging from underground. But she had no clear idea about most of the dates—had he fought the Pechenegs before the Bulgarians, and what about Robert Guiscard and his handsome blond son, Bohemond? When had Alexios fought the Turks, or rather, when had he not been fighting the Turks? What of the Franks and their Crusade? She had been a child in those years and had no clear recollection of the particulars, except perhaps of the dashing Bohemond, whose attentions had so flattered her.

Anna leaned back in her chair, trying to recall dates and places, vexed at her inability to remember even the meanest description of them. It was then that she glanced at the box of her husband's papers, his unfinished history of Alexios's reign she had brought with her to the monastery after his death. Perhaps they held that information.

Sister Irene looked quizzically at her, awaiting a response.

"Sister, it has been so long I cannot recall exactly when my father fought his battles," she said in apology. "Let me retrieve some notes my husband made. He served in my father's army and was writing a history of him when he died."

Anna walked over to the shelf where her husband's wooden box had sat since her arrival, sealed tightly with a leather strap buckled around it, a gray film of dust covering it. She blew the dust off, loosened the strap, and removed the lid. She scanned the first sheet of the expensive, stiff parchment. It told of a disastrous battle against the Norman, Robert Guiscard, and his marauding soldiers at Dyrrhachium soon after Alexios took the throne, an unfortunate occasion for her father. Her glance flickered toward Sister Irene, and she put that sheet aside.

"Umm, I don't believe my husband quite finished this one," came Anna's glib explanation for putting aside that page. She continued searching. *No soldier wins all his battles*, she thought, *but no need to start Alexios's story with a rout.* The next sheet in the box recounted a victory over the Pechenegs, a more pleasing topic for their discussion. Satisfied, Anna brought the parchment to the table, where she and Sister Irene perused it for the rest of that hour.

Afterward, Anna did not return to refectory with Irene. Instead, she retrieved more of the sheets and spent the rest of the day reading them. The leaves were filled with details she had never known about Alexios's military campaigns. Anna's husband had died while on a diplomatic mission for her brother, leaving his history of Alexios's reign incomplete.

The stiff parchment had scrapes where he had made changes, lacunae that needed completion. She picked up more of them, reading her husband's descriptions of Alexios's many battles and victories when the two had fought together. Her husband's writings told of the tactics and strategies her father had used in his many battles and wars. But they were somehow incomplete, not the polished prose of a true history. Their dull rendition of military details lacked the lively spark of the man who had so inspired his soldiers' loyalty and led to his heroic rise to the throne, aided by the plotting of his fearless mother, Anna Dalassena.

Dusk found her still sitting at the desk by the window in the fading light. She recalled her first conversation with Sister Irene in the garden by the stunted rosebush on her birthday months earlier. She wondered if her father would be forgotten, the memory of him swept away in the storms of time, never to be recalled. Worse, would the memory of her accursed brother's reign even overshadow that of Alexios's? She shuddered at that preposterous thought but knew too well the fawning scholars who wrote histories and flocked to court.

Her fingers drummed on the table next to the bright polished silver oil lamp the serving girl had lit, an idea taking shape in her mind. She ran a slim freckled finger along the edge of the box where her unused quills lay, waiting to be dipped in ink. Her heart began beating faster, roused by new determination.

***

In the morning, a warm wind blew up from the south, a breath of the approaching spring filling the air. The sun still hung low in the sky, a misty nimbus surrounding it, softening its brilliance. Salty sea air blew in its fishy odor from the docks on the Golden Horn.

A shaft of pale morning sunlight fell on the diminutive rosebush Anna had noticed that winter's day months earlier. Her mother had been right about it. It needed a sunnier spot where it could grow and flower as it was meant to. She retrieved a spade from the shed where the garden tools lay and returned to the flowerbed. She quickly dug up the small plant that had lived so long in shadows and moved it into the open where the sun could reach it. The languishing rosebush needed to move only a few footsteps within the monastery's walls to bloom. Gazing on the replanted bush, she knew her life at Kecharitomene must change too.

Anna returned to her rooms, washed, and sat again at her desk. Her husband's unfinished notes lay before her alongside empty sheets of parchment awaiting ink. Her life was not over, even if she was confined inside these red brick walls. She lived and breathed and thought—and she would spend her remaining days writing her father's history. She would earn the respect of Constantinople's scholars, and finally gain Alexios's and Irene's approval, if only in the afterlife. She took up the waiting quill, dipped it in the inkpot, and began, "The stream of time, ever moving . . ."

Author's Note:

Anna Comnena (1083-1153) was the firstborn child of the Byzantine Emperor Alexios I Comnenus and his wife, the Empress Irene Ducaena. She was betrothed at birth to Constantine Ducas, the son of a previous ruler, the Emperor Michael VII

Ducas and his wife, the lovely Empress Maria of Alan. The original intention was for Anna and Constantine to succeed Alexios on the throne, and Anna was at first raised with this expectation. However, Constantine took ill and died, and Alexios and Irene gave birth to many more children, including the son who would become his father's successor and Anna Comnena's nemesis, her brother John II Comnenus.

John was a beloved and well-regarded ruler despite his sister's envious disdain. Still, it could be argued that Anna Comnena, after spending the last fifteen years of her life writing a still respected history of her father's reign, *The Alexiad*, is now the better remembered of the two. Perhaps, in this case, history was told not by the victor, but by the writer.

Acknowledgements

John Julius Norwich's <u>A Short History of Byzantium</u> planted the seed that blossomed into my obsession with the Byzantines. I will be forever grateful to him for that small book. He has said he considers himself to be 'just' a popularizer of history, but that book was magical for me. I can heartily recommend it, or for the more intrepid, his three-volume masterpiece, <u>Byzantium,</u> if you are looking for an enjoyable overview of Byzantine history.

I must also express my gratitude to the first readers who laid eyes on the stories, the talented writers A.X. Ahmad and Tinney Sue Heath, and my Goodreads friend, Jane Rawoof. Their suggestions helped immeasurably as I toiled away on my computer each evening.

My editor and creative cover designer, Jennifer Toney Quinlan, provided valuable insights, advice, and encouragement, as well as a striking cover for this collection. I could not have done this without her.

Finally, to my husband, Kenneth, and daughters Melissa, Suzanne and Kathleen – thank you for your patience as I holed up nights and weekends with my writing for so long.

About the Author

Eileen Stephenson was born in Fort Worth, Texas, but has spent most of her life in the Washington, D.C. area, earning a living in the finance industry before discovering the enthralling world of the Byzantines. She has degrees from Georgetown University and George Washington University and is married with three daughters.

Final Note

Reviews are critical for all authors, but especially for those like myself who are just starting out. If you enjoyed this collection of stories (and even if you didn't), please consider leaving a review at Amazon, Barnes & Noble, Goodreads or other reader websites you might frequent. Learning what readers like or don't like is the only way to get better.

Please visit my website,

eileenstephenson.com

and sign up to hear about my upcoming release – _Imperial Passions._

Made in the USA
Middletown, DE
07 May 2015